Lemons NEVER LIE

by **Richard Stark**

A HARD CASE CRIME NOVEL

A HARD CASE CRIME BOOK
(HCC-022)
July 2006

Published by

Dorchester Publishing Co., Inc.
200 Madison Avenue
New York, NY 10016

in collaboration with Winterfall LLC

ISBN 0-8439-5594-5

The name "Hard Case Crime" and the Hard Case Crime logo are trademarks of Winterfall LLC. Hard Case Crime books are selected and edited by Charles Ardai.

Printed in the United States of America

Visit us on the web at www.HardCaseCrime.com

This is for Edgar Carreras,
wherever he may be.

Las Vegas

I

Grofield put a nickel in the slot machine, pulled the lever, and watched a lemon, a lemon, and a lemon come up. The machine coughed fourteen nickels into the chrome tray. Grofield frowned at them; what the hell do you do with fourteen nickels? Besides bag your suit.

A happy stout woman of fifty in Easter Sunday clothes—pale blue—and carrying a black raincoat, a lavender umbrella, a red and white shopping bag, a blue airline bag, and a large black imitation alligator purse paused to say, "You're very lucky, young man. You're going to really sock it to 'em here."

Grofield never watched television, and therefore didn't know the woman was quoting a popular line of the day. He took the statement at face value, as a result, and just looked at her for a second, astounded that a woman who looked like that would say such a weird thing.

A thin farmerish man with a chicken neck was with the woman. "Come on, Edna," he said, irritably. "We gotta get the bags." He was carrying a camera case, a shopping bag, and an airline bag.

The woman said to him, "Didn't you see what this young man did? Now, that's what I call luck. Steps off the plane, plays the slot machine once, and look what he wins. That's what I do call luck."

"Bad luck," Grofield said, and pointed. "Lemons. You know what they say about lemons."

"Nooo," said the woman, and looked roguish. "But I know what they say about Chinese girls!" She was really on vacation.

The man said, "Come *on*, Edna."

Grofield shook his head, looking at the lemons. "I hate to use the luck up all at once. It's a bad sign."

The woman, while still looking happy, also now looked a little puzzled. "But you won!" she said. The other passengers were streaming by, down the gauntlet of slot machines from the plane to the baggage area and the taxis. None of them stopped at the machines, though a lot of them smiled and looked excited and pointed the machines out to one another.

Grofield shook his head at the lemons once more, and turned to say to the woman, "I don't gamble. Every time I come to this town, I put a nickel in one of these machines on the way in, and another nickel in on the way out. I think of it as dues. They never tried to give me back my dues before, and I consider it a bad sign."

"You don't *gamble?*" In her home town, she would have given the same reading to the sentence, "You don't go to *church?*" She was one hundred percent on vacation.

"Not if I can help it," Grofield said.

"Then what do you come to Las Vegas for?"

Grofield grinned and winked. "That's a secret," he said. "Bye, now." He turned and started away.

The woman called, "You left your money!"

He looked back, and she was pointing at the fourteen nickels in the trough. "That's not *my* money," he said. "It belongs to the machine."

"But you *won* it!"

Grofield considered telling her it was seventy cents.

He shook his head, and said, "Then I give it to you. Welcome to our city." He waved, and walked on.

At the far end, where the corridor curved to the right, he glanced back and saw the couple standing back there in front of the machine. Their goods were stacked in a semicircle around them like an impromptu fortress. The woman's right hand was pushing the nickels in and pulling the lever down. Grofield walked on.

He had to wait ten minutes for his suitcase. When he got it, he turned away toward the taxis and saw the chicken-necked man getting change at an airline counter. Feeling a little guilty, Grofield went out and joined the passengers waiting for cabs.

2

The wrestler in the turtleneck shirt patted Grofield all over, while Grofield stood with legs slightly apart and arms extended straight out at his sides, like an illustration in an exercise book. The wrestler had bad breath. Grofield didn't suggest anything to him, and after a minute the frisk was done and the wrestler said, "Okay, you're clean."

"Naturally," Grofield said. "I came here to talk."

The wrestler made no response. He'd been hired as a doorman, and that was it. "They're in the other room," he said.

Grofield went on into the other room, feeling pessimistic. First the three lemons at the airport, and now this. Myers, the organizer of this thing and a man Grofield didn't know, had set himself up in a two-room suite in the tower section of one of the Strip hotels. Why would a man spend so much money on a meeting place? Why meet in Las Vegas in the first place? It hinted of a blowhard somewhere in the tapestry.

Grofield hoped not. He wasn't going to permit his need to interfere with his common sense and his professional judgment, but the fact was, his need was great. Mary was back home in Indiana, sleeping on the stage. This trip was taking most of Grofield's available capital, after a season of summer stock that any conglomerate would have been happy to have for their tax loss. If Myers turned out not to have anything, there were going to be some lean winter days until something *did* appear.

A member of an increasingly disappearing breed of professionals, Alan Grofield was an actor who limited himself to live performances before live audiences. Movies and television were for mannequins, not actors. An actor who stepped before a camera was in the process of rotting his own talent. Instead of learning to build a performance through three acts—or five, if the season is classical—he learns facile reactions in snippets of make believe.

No purist can hope to do well financially, whatever his field, and Grofield was no exception. Not only did he limit his acting to the live theater, where the demand for actors declines still further every year, but he insisted on running his own theaters, usually summer stock, frequently in out-of-the-way places and invariably at a loss. To support himself, therefore, he from time to time turned to his second profession, as he was doing now.

He stepped into the second room, closing the door after him, and looked around at the three men already in the room. He knew none of them. "I'm Grofield," he said.

The florid-faced man in the ascot and madras jacket came over from the window, hand outstretched, saying, "I'm Myers." He had an Eastern-boarding-school accent, the sort that sounds affected but isn't. "So glad you could come."

Grofield, not entirely believing the situation, shook the hand of the man who was supposed to be masterminding the robbery. Everything was wrong so far, the lemons had not lied.

Who *was* Myers? He couldn't be a professional. He

now took Grofield around and introduced him to the other two. "This is Cathcart, he'll be driving one of the cars. George Cathcart, Alan Grofield."

In Cathcart's eyes, Grofield detected a guarded echo of his own bewilderment, and by an infinitesimal measure he relaxed. At least there were *some* professionals here. He took Cathcart's hand in honest pleasure, and they nodded at one another.

Cathcart was a stocky man, short, with the broad low tugboat build that most good getaway drivers seem to have. He had obviously tried to dress himself to match his surroundings, but that brown suit wouldn't have belonged in this hotel even when it was new. And wherever it was Cathcart usually lived, did men really wear black shoes and white socks with brown suits? Possibly Newark, New Jersey.

Myers was pushing on, like a garden party hostess. "And this is Matt Hanto, our explosives man."

Explosives men tend to be built like a stick of dynamite, long and lean, and Matt Hanto was no exception. He would probably have been a state finalist in a national Gary Cooper Lookalike Contest. He peered at Grofield as though squinting at him across miles of sun-blasted desert, and solemnly shook hands.

"Only two to go," Myers said. "While we're waiting, would you care for anything?" He gestured like a sales manager at a table loaded with an assortment of bottles and glasses and two of the hotel's plastic ice buckets.

"No, thanks," Grofield said. "Not on duty." And the connecting door to the wrestler's room opened and Dan Leach came in. Grofield looked at him, pleased to see a face he knew, and at the same time wishing there were some way to take Dan aside and ask for a briefing on all this. He was here by Dan's invitation, after all, and on the phone Dan hadn't said anything about this being other than a normal gig. Of course, nobody ever said much on the phone in any event, but still.

Dan was tall like Matt Hanto and broad like George Cathcart and utterly without a sense of humor. He came in now, leaving the intervening door open, and said to Myers, "Your friend is taking a nap."

Myers looked blank. "I beg your pardon?"

Dan jabbed a thumb over his shoulder and walked away from the open door. While Myers hurried over in bewilderment to look through the doorway, Dan walked up to Grofield and said, "How've you been?"

"Fine." They didn't bother to shake hands, they already knew each other.

Dan said, "You put up with that?"

"With what? The frisk?" Grofield shrugged. "I figured, what the hell."

"You're more easygoing than I am." Dan said, and Myers popped back into the room to say, loudly, "You knocked him out!"

Dan turned and looked at him. "I came here to listen to a project," he said. "Not to get shaken down."

"Dan, I've got to protect myself. I know you, but I don't know these other boys."

"If that's the best help you can find," Dan said, "you might as well surrender. What's that, booze?" He walked over to the bar-table.

Myers stood there, near the doorway, watching Dan go and trying to figure out what to say or do next. Grofield, watching him, was more than ever sure the lemons had told him the truth. He should never have left the airport. Fourteen nickels—he could have killed the time until another plane was ready to leave, going anywhere.

Before Myers could come up with a response, a sixth man walked in, saying, "There's a gent bleeding from the nose in the other room. I'm Frith, Bob Frith. The gent seems to be alive."

Myers was playing out of his class, but he had fairly good recuperative powers. He grabbed the interruption and ran with it. "That's another problem, Bob," he said, "and nothing for us to worry about. Come on in, I'm Andrew Myers." Taking Frith's hand in one of his hands, he used the other to swing the connecting door shut. "Now we're all here," Myers said, pulling Frith farther into the room, away from the door and the implications of what lay beyond it. "Now, we'll just introduce ourselves, and we can get started."

There was very little introducing left to be done. While Myers did it, Dan came back across the room to stand beside Grofield again, this time with a glass in his hand. Dan seemed casual and easygoing, but in fact he was rigid and unshakable. His total self-confidence came across as blandness, and frequently led people to underestimate him.

Now, while Myers was introducing people to each other on the far side of the room, Grofield said, "What is all this, Dan?"

Dan shrugged. "A maybe. We can talk about it later."

Myers was obviously self-conscious, and Grofield and Dan talking together was making him nervous. Now he finished with his introductions and came to the middle of the room and said, "Everybody take a seat, or stand if you want, uh, whatever you want to do." He grinned painfully and said, "The smoking lamp is lit." He'd apparently hoped that was going to be a joke; when nobody laughed he started blinking a lot, and became briskly businesslike. "I have the presentation here," he said, and quickly pulled a suitcase out from under the bed.

Grofield looked at Dan, but Dan was facing front, watching Myers with no particular expression on his face. Grofield decided the only thing to do was wait it out, so he also faced front, and watched Myers put the suitcase on the bed, unlock it, put his key ring back in his pants pocket, and open the suitcase.

Myers said, "Now, you boys may not believe this, but what we're talking about here is a payroll job." He turned away from the suitcase to flash a bright smile around at everybody. "I know what you're thinking," he said.

Grofield almost said something, but restrained himself.

Myers said, "You're thinking there are no payroll jobs anymore. You're thinking there isn't a payroll in the country of any size that isn't done by check these days. But there is at least one, and I know where it is and how to get at it."

The suitcase Myers had opened was of the rigid type, and the top was now standing straight up. Myers reached into the suitcase and picked up a piece of stiff cardboard almost as long and wide as the suitcase itself, and propped it against the top. It was a blow-up color photograph of a factory building on a sunny day. The building was old, made of brick, and surrounded by fairly dirty snow.

"Here it is," Myers said. "Northway Brewery, Monequois, New York. Right near the Canadian border. They used to do their payroll by check, but the union was against it. They have a lot of Canadians working there, a lot of backwoodsmen and so on, and they want their money in cash. They pay weekly, and the average payroll is in the area of a hundred twenty thousand dollars."

Grofield automatically did the math. Six men. Twenty thousand each. Not very much, but enough to get him into the next season if he were careful with it. He began to hope the lemons would turn out to be wrong, after all.

Myers was reaching for another piece of cardboard, this one turning out to contain a map. "As you can see, Monequois is less than five miles from the border. That makes a nice escape route for us. We have our choice of these three highways—here, here, and here—all going north. There are secondary roads that bypass the customs stations at the border." Another piece of cardboard; another photograph. "Now, this is the main gate. The money is delivered on Friday mornings at ten or ten-thirty."

Myers went on describing where the money came from, how it was guarded, how it was paid out, and the more he talked the tougher the job sounded. The money, which came every week from Buffalo via Watertown, was heavily guarded every step of the way, including police helicopter reconnaissance on the armored car that drove it from Watertown to the factory. The factory itself was at least half fort, with a high brick wall around the perimeter of the grounds, topped by barbed wire, and with only two entrances, both well guarded. Grofield glanced at Dan two or three times during Myers' recital, but Dan's expression of patient attention never changed.

Finally Myers got to the operation itself. "I've cleared

it with the Outfit," he said. "They want ten percent, which seems perfectly all right to me."

Matt Hanto, the explosives man, said, "Who the hell are you talkin' about?"

Myers looked surprised. "The Outfit," he said. "You know, the Syndicate."

"You mean the Mafia?"

"Well, I don't know if it's Mafia up in that neck of the woods, but they're all interconnected with each other around the country, aren't they?"

George Cathcart, driver, said, "You want us to give ten percent off the top to the local mob?"

"Well, naturally," Myers said.

"For what?"

"For protection," Myers said, as though he was telling them something everybody knew. "For permission to work in their territory."

Bob Frith, the other driver, said, "You're out of your mind, Mr. Myers. I never asked nobody permission in my life."

Myers looked astonished. "You want to go into that town without clearing things with the local people?"

He was going to get a lot of answers to that, but Dan Leach short-circuited them all, saying, "Let's forget about that, for a minute. I'm more interested how you figure we're going to *get* this payroll. We'll split it up later."

Myers was just as glad for the change of subject. "Fine," he said. "Good idea. Now, it'll take two vehicles, a fire engine and a regular car. The fire engine to do the job, and the car to make the getaway. Now, here's the Municipal Services Building of the town of

Monequois—" And damned if he didn't have yet another blow-up photograph to show them. That was about ten photos and maps and graphs so far; Grofield was beginning to feel like a man who'd stumbled by mistake into a lecture on auto safety.

But Myers wasn't interested in auto safety, or any other kind of safety either. His plan, once he started outlining it, was a dilly. The police and fire departments of the town of Monequois were together in the same building; Myers' first step would be to blow up that building. Simultaneously, there would be an incendiary explosion—that is, an explosion followed hopefully by a fire—at the Northway Brewery. Naturally, no gate guard would think of stopping a fire engine from coming through the brewery's main gate with a fire going on. Frith would drive the fire engine, and Grofield and Dan Leach would ride it in firemen's uniforms. They would stop outside the paymaster's office, and Grofield and Leach would spray the office with machine gun bullets, killing the guards inside. Then they would—

"No," said Grofield.

Myers stopped in mid-sentence, his hand dipping down for yet another photo or map or graph. He blinked. "What?"

"I said no. Don't tell me any more of it, I'm out."

Myers frowned; he couldn't understand it. "What's the matter, Grofield?"

"Killing," Grofield said.

"They've got half a dozen armed guards in there," Myers said. "There's absolutely no other way to get past them."

"I believe you. That's why I'm out."

Myers looked sardonic. "You really that kind, Grofield? Sight of blood bother you?"

"No, it's more the sight of cops. The law looks a lot harder for a killer than it does for a thief. Sorry, Myers, but you can count me out."

Grofield turned toward the door. Behind him, he heard Dan Leach say, "Thanks for the drink."

Myers' voice sounded shocked: "You, too?"

Grofield opened the door and stepped through into the other room. He felt Dan coming along behind him, and heard Dan close the door on Myers' calling voice and on the other voices also starting up.

The wrestler was lying face down on the floor, on his right cheek. He was unconscious, and his nose had stopped bleeding.

Grofield said, "You really hit them, don't you?"

"Only when they ask."

They went out to the hall and headed for the elevators. Grofield said, "Now, will you tell me who that madman is and how you rung me in on it?"

"He's a friend of my wife's brother," Dan said. "He's supposed to of done some stuff down around Texas."

"He's a simpleton," Grofield said.

3

The dice ricocheted from the backboard, bounced back on two separate trajectories across the green felt and came up three and four. The shooter groaned, money changed hands, and the dice passed to Dan Leach. "Operate the numbers for me," he said, and Grofield said, "Sure."

You couldn't get out of one of these Strip hotels without going through the casino. Grofield wasn't a gambling man, but Dan was, so on the way by he'd said, "Let's earn us our plane fare anyway."

"Not me."

"Well, I will. Hang in and watch, and take the free drinks."

Grofield had nothing to do until he took another plane out of here tomorrow, so he'd stayed. Dan obviously had played on a Las Vegas-style layout before, and he'd been picking up a few dollars on the other shooters' rolls. Now he had a chance on his own roll.

"For the boys," he said, to begin with, and dropped a one dollar chip on the six-five come. If he rolled an eleven, the four housemen it took to work this table would split the fifteen dollars that bet would win; if he rolled any other number, that dollar would be lost.

"Thank you for the chance, sir," said the stickman neutrally, and pushed Dan the dice; red translucent plastic with large white dots.

Dan rolled the dice between both palms, to warm

them. He had the slightly loose smile on his face that has nothing to do with humor, but that means the player feels at home, his adrenalin is pumping. He held the dice in his right hand, shook once, and threw.

Six-two.

"The point is eight," said the stickman, and drew the dice back down the table to Dan.

Dan said to Grofield, "Cover the numbers."

"Right."

Across from Grofield, in six squares imprinted on the felt were the numbers *4 5 6 8 9* and *10*. A round black thing something like a hockey puck had been put by the houseman there over the *8* square; that was the shooter's number, and could not be bet. Grofield put three dollars of Dan's chips on each of the other numbers. If he rolled one of those numbers before rolling either his point—eight—or losing with a seven, the house would pay off on that number. No bet would be lost on any of those numbers until he either won or lost his try to make his point; the money could ride, roll after roll.

"Keep 'em covered," Dan said, rolling the dice around between his palms again. "I feel a long roll coming on."

"I'm on it," Grofield promised.

Dan proceeded to roll thirty-four times without either a seven or an eight coming up. Twice in the course of it he had Grofield up the bets covering the five numbers, the second time to fifteen dollars each. On the thirty-fifth roll, the dice did their jig and wound up four-four. The lady across the way with twenty-five dollars on the hard way blew Dan a kiss, and he winked at her. The houseman inspected the dice again—he'd been inspecting them every four or five rolls—and another houseman pushed the rest of Dan's winnings to him. It made a messy mountain at his corner of the table.

Dan said to Grofield, "Cover don't–come for me. I'm through. I can feel it."

"Done."

Dan threw a five. Grofield covered don't–come, and Dan threw a seven. He won some and he lost some. "That's it," he said. He passed the dice to the red-haired man to his left, and he and Grofield filled their pockets with chips and went over to the cashier's window to turn them in.

It came to twelve-thousand eight-hundred dollars. Dan looked at his watch and said, "An hour and ten minutes. That's not bad wages."

"Not at all," Grofield said.

Dan looked at him, stuffing money away. "You don't gamble at all?"

Grofield thought of the fourteen nickels. "Sometimes I take a whirl," he admitted. "I never had a night like you, though."

"I believe I'll go back to the hotel and pack," Dan said. "Nice to see you again."

"Sure. You hear of anything else, keep me in mind."

"That I will."

They went outside and took separate cabs to their separate small-time motels far from the Strip.

4

They kicked the lock off the door and came in with their hands full of shotguns. Two of them, in black hats and anonymous black raincoats with the collars turned up. Also black handkerchiefs across their faces, like stage-coach robbers.

Grofield had been sitting there going over a play he thought they might do this summer. He'd come back to the motel, got himself a bite to eat, called the airport to arrange for a morning flight to Indianapolis via St. Louis, and had been sitting there ever since with the yellow-jacketed Samuel French edition of the play open on the writing desk in front of him. Then they kicked the lock off the door and came in and pointed shotguns at him, and he dropped his red pencil, put his hands up in the air, and said, "I'm on your side."

"On your feet," the tall one said. The other one was shorter and fatter.

Grofield got to his feet. He kept his hands over his head.

The tall one kept a shotgun pointed at him while the short one searched the room. He went through Grofield's suitcase, and the closet, and the bureau drawers. Then he searched Grofield. Grofield recoiled slightly; the guy had bad breath.

Finally the short one stepped back and picked his shotgun off the bed and said, "It isn't here."

The tall one said to Grofield, "Where is it?"

"I don't know."

"Don't waste time, Jack, we're not playin' a game."

"I didn't think you were. Not with guns, and kicking the door in and all. But I don't know what you're looking for, so I don't know where it is."

"Ho-ho," said the tall one. It didn't sound very much like a laugh. "You won almost thirteen grand tonight," he said.

"Sorry," Grofield said. "Not me."

"You," the tall one said. "Cough it up."

"You got your choice," the short one said. "You can be alive and poor, or dead and rich."

"I'm sorry," Grofield said. "I hate to be killed because of somebody else's mistake, but I didn't win any money tonight."

They looked at one another. The short one said, "We picked the wrong one."

"We *followed* the wrong one," the tall one said, as though the correction were important.

"Yeah, that's what I meant," the short one said. He turned back to Grofield. "Turn around," he said. "Face the wall."

Grofield turned around and faced the wall. He knew what was coming, and hunched his head down into his neck, trying to make his skull soft and resilient. It didn't do any good. The lights went out very painfully.

5

"I'm drowning!" Grofield yelled, and thrashed his arms around, trying to swim; his nose was full of water.

"You aren't drowning, you bastard. Wake up."

Grofield woke up. He rubbed water from his face, opened his eyes, and looked up at the angry face of Dan Leach. "Christ," he said.

"Not even close," Dan said. "Sit up."

Grofield lifted his head, and the back of it made a commotion like it was glued to the floor. "Ow," Grofield said. He snorted water out of his mouth, and wiped his face with his sleeve. "My head."

"Your head. My dough. Do you sit up, or do I beat the crap out of you right here?"

"Beat the crap out of me right here," Grofield said. "I hurt too much to sit up."

Doubt creased Dan's forehead. "Are you putting me on?"

Grofield had gently touched his fingertips to the back of his head, and hadn't liked it at all. Now he looked at his hand and saw brownish-red smears on the balls of his fingers. "Sure I'm putting you on," he said, and turned his hand around to show it to Dan. "You want ketchup for your hamburger?"

Dan was having trouble changing from a conviction he'd been happy with. "If it wasn't you," he said, "how'd they get to me?"

"You'll have to give me a minute on questions like that."

"Listen, let me get you up on the bed."

"Who's fighting?"

Dan picked him up, and Grofield tried to keep his head from flopping around. Dan put him down on the bed and said, "Can you roll over on your side? I wanna see your head."

"Sure," Grofield said. He rolled over, and bitterly studied the wall while Dan was out of sight, seeing to his head.

Dan said, "A cut, that's all…not deep." He touched Grofield's head, which stung like fury. "Nothing broken. It'll hurt, though."

"You sure?"

"Definitely," Dan said. He had no sense of humor at all. He said, "Roll back over now, we got to talk."

Grofield rolled back over. Dan pulled up a chair, as though he were a visitor in a hospital, and sat there with his elbows on the edge of the bed. His face was very close to Grofield's. He said, "You wanna know what happened to me?"

Grofield moved his head slightly so he could see Dan with both eyes and said, "Two guys in raincoats and shotguns took your money away."

"That's right."

"They were here, too."

"I know that," Dan said. "They thought it was funny. They picked the wrong guy first, followed you home instead of me."

"Very funny," Grofield said.

"But then they corrected their mistake," Dan said.

"I know."

"And that's what I got to thank *you* for," Dan said. "Head or no head, blood or no blood, that's still what I got to thank *you* for."

"You think I sent them to you?"

"Who else? What other way are they gonna get to me? They followed *you*, they didn't follow me. The only way they get to me is if you tell them where I'm staying."

"Wrong," Grofield said.

"What do you mean, wrong? They followed *you*, not—"

"No, they didn't."

Dan frowned, trying very hard to understand. "Cough it out," he said.

"They didn't follow anybody," Grofield said. "Didn't you recognize them? It was Myers and the guy you knocked out."

Dan stared. "Are you crazy?"

"They muffled their voices behind those masks," Grofield said, "But I recognized them anyway. The bouncer, at any rate." He wrinkled his nose in distaste.

"You're sure it was them."

"I know definitely it was them. Even if I didn't recognize them, and I did, I know I didn't tell them where you were staying. They didn't even ask. The fat one said something about picking the wrong one, and Myers told him he meant they'd *followed* the wrong one. Trying to cover a slip of the tongue."

"They hijacked me," Dan said, as though he couldn't believe it. "Called me here to this lousy town for a caper, come up with a heist out of the comic books, and then hijack *me*."

"That's right."

Dan got to his feet. "They need to learn some things," he said. He was suddenly in a hurry to go somewhere.

"Manners, for instance," Grofield said. Experimentally he lifted his head from the pillow, and it didn't seem to hurt as much.

"I've gotta go talk to them," Dan said, and turned toward the door. The lock was still broken, but the door had been pushed all the way closed.

"Hold on," Grofield said. He sat up, a bit shaky. "I'll come with you. I'd like to talk to those birds myself."

"You're in no shape to go anywhere," Dan said.

"There's two of them, there should be two of you. Give me five minutes."

"Five minutes?" Dan was so impatient he was practically tapdancing.

"If they're gonna check out tonight," Grofield said, "they've done it by now. If they're gonna wait till morning, you can afford five minutes. Go get me some ice."

"You wanna *drink?*"

"I want to put it on the back of my head," Grofield said, patiently.

"Oh. Sure."

Dan went out—the door made unhappy rending noises whenever it was moved—and Grofield went shakily into the bathroom to soak his head and grit his teeth.

6

Grofield opened the closet door and the wrestler smiled up at him with his slit throat. "Here he is," Grofield called, and Dan came in from the other room saying, "Which one? Let me get my hands on him."

Grofield stepped back, and Dan looked at the thing on the floor of the closet. "Jesus," he said.

"Your friend Myers," Grofield said, "is around the bend."

"He cut his throat for six grand," Dan said. He sounded awed.

"He was going to kill everybody in New York State for one-sixth of a hundred grand," Grofield said.

"I can't believe he's so penny ante," Dan said. He looked at Grofield and shook his head. "That's what gets me. He was supposed to be such hot shit down there in Texas."

Grofield said, "He's left us a mess. You remember everything you touched?"

"Good Christ on a crutch!" Dan looked around. "This room, the next room. I had a drink in there, when he was showing us all those pictures. We've *all* got prints scattered around in there."

"Do a fast wipe," Grofield said. "That's all we have time for."

"Maybe what we want is a fire."

"No. It would just call attention to this room earlier than necessary, and it wouldn't destroy things like doorknobs."

Dan was still agitated. He looked at the thing in the closet again and said, "Maybe we oughta move him. Carry him out like he's drunk, dump him somewheres."

"Forget it, Dan," Grofield said. He went over to the bed and pulled a pillowcase off its pillow. "He's all over blood," he said. "Here, catch." He tossed the crumpled pillowcase, and turned away to reach for the other pillow before waiting to see if Dan had caught it or not. "We'll wipe the place down," he said, shaking the pillow out. "That's all we have time for."

"All right," Dan said. He sounded doubtful, but willing to be led.

They spent the next five minutes wiping hard surfaces in the two rooms. Myers had cleared out with his goods, including the suitcase full of maps and photos and graphs. Grofield, wiping glasses, said, "You think he still means to pull that factory job?"

"He doesn't have time," Dan said. He sounded grim.

The last thing they wiped was the inside doorknob. Out in the hall, Grofield wiped the outside doorknob with his jacket sleeve, and the two of them walked down to the elevators.

"I hate it that I have to go after that bastard," Dan said. "I got other things to do with my life."

"Then let it ride," Grofield said. "If you ever meet up with him again, you'll take care of things. If not, it didn't cost you anything."

"Over twelve grand."

"I don't count gambling winnings as money," Grofield said, and shrugged. They'd reached the elevators; he pushed the down button.

"I count money as money," Dan said.

"I guess I don't blame you," Grofield admitted.

The elevator came. It had three passengers already, so they didn't talk any more until they reached the main floor.

Walking around toward the lobby, Dan said, "You remember the names of any of those other guys?"

"Up with Myers? Bob Frith, George Cathcart, Matt Hanto."

"Wait a second." Dan brought out a ballpoint pen and a crumpled envelope. Grofield repeated the names, and Dan wrote them down. He put the pen and envelope away and said, "You know any of them from anywhere?"

"No. Don't you?"

"They looked all right," Dan said. "They looked like pros. Somebody'll know them, in the business."

"They weren't in on it," Grofield said. "That was strictly Myers and his fat friend, I'm sure of it."

"I know, I know. But one of the others might know where I can get in touch with him."

"Ask your wife's brother."

"I will, don't you worry. I'll ask him a *lot* of things."

They were going through the casino. Grofield nodded at the crap tables: "You want to get it back again?"

But Dan shook his head. "My luck is gone for tonight," he said. "I can feel it."

They went on outside. Cabdrivers looked alert at their exit. Dan said, "You want to come with me?"

"To find Myers?"

"Sure."

"For what?"

Dan shrugged. "Half."

"Six grand?" Grofield considered it, then shook his

head. "Too much like work," he said. "You don't know how long it'll take, you don't know if you'll ever find him at all."

"Still, I got to try."

"Good luck," Grofield said.

"Thanks."

"And if you hear of anything in my line, let me know."

"I will."

They took separate cabs again, and when he got to his room Grofield found his luggage gone. Naturally; it had been possible to close the door, but not lock it.

"Lemons don't lie," Grofield said bitterly, and went away to the motel office to report the theft. Not that he expected the cops to find the stolen luggage; a resort town like this was always full of crooks. But at least he'd get the tax deduction.

Mead Grove, Indiana

I

Grofield put his shoulder against the door and pushed, and slowly it rolled back, and early April sunlight angled through to shine on the dusty wood floor of the stage. The door was wood, with *X* framing on both sides, and was eight feet high and eight feet wide. It was suspended from a track over the doorway by nine greasy little wheels, most of which squeaked as Grofield kept pushing, leaning his shoulder into the old wood and plodding steadily forward, opening the door against its sullen will.

It was three weeks now since he'd come back from Las Vegas, and the phone hadn't rung once with a job offer. He was really sorry Myers and the factory payroll had turned out to be no good; Mary was down in town now, working at the supermarket for eating money. They were supposed to open this damn theater for the summer season in two and a half months, and where the money was coming from Grofield had no idea.

It was a long eight feet, with the door resisting every inch of the way, but at last the eight-foot-square opening was completely cleared. Grofield kicked the wooden wedge under the end of the door to keep it from rolling closed again, and turned to look at his theater in sunlight.

It wasn't very much. The building had been a barn originally, for the first seventy years of its life or so, and at some point in the first decade after World War II someone had converted it into a summer theater, putting the stage in at this end, and raising the floor out there where the audience sat by putting in a series of platforms, so that the first four rows of seats were down on the original barn floor, the next four rows were on a platform two steps up from that, the next four rows two more steps up, and so on. There were twenty-four rows in all, ten seats across, with a center aisle. Two hundred forty seats. Three or four times, Grofield had actually seen them all full.

This was a hell of a part of the world for a summer theater, that was the problem. The only thing in Indiana big enough to find blindfolded is Indianapolis, and once you've found *that* there's nothing to do with it. And even if there were, Mead Grove was too far away from it to matter. There were no tourist areas nearby, no major cities, no university towns. The only potential customers were the residents of Mead Grove and the other half-dozen small towns in the area, and the farmers in between. Most of them weren't quite sure what a live theater was for, and doubted it was anything they wanted to know any more about. If it weren't for schoolteachers and doctors' wives, there wouldn't have been any audience at all.

The upshot was that the forgotten nut who'd converted the barn to a summer theater twenty years ago had promptly lost his shirt—and the barn. It had changed hands several times in the last two decades; had briefly been a barn again for a while; had been a movie theater even more briefly; had been a warehouse for a bicycle parts manufacturer, who had gone broke for reasons other than his ownership of this building; and had several times been a financially disastrous summer theater. And finally, three years ago, Alan Grofield had bought the building and twelve acres of land around it, including two small farmhouses, with most of the money he'd brought back from an island casino heist he'd worked with a guy named Parker. He'd bought the place outright, no mortgage, and told himself that from now on he'd have roots, he'd have a place where he belonged and where he could always come home to. He'd known in front that the summer theater would lose money, but it hadn't bothered him; summer theaters always lose money, particularly when run by actors, and most particularly when not placed along one of the coasts of the United States. But the theater wasn't supposed to be a living, it was supposed to be a way of life, and that was different. His *living* was working with men like Parker—and Dan Leach.

But not men like Myers.

And, in fact, nobody at all for a while now. He'd gotten into another job with Parker, an armored car thing, but it had gone badly and Grofield had come very close to a jail term. Since then, nothing much had happened. Two seasons of stock had drained away most of his savings, and now here he was less than three months from the third season and he just didn't have the money to put the thing together. Even if he stuck with revivals, meaning plays in the public domain that he didn't have to pay an author any performance fee on, there were still expenses; housing and feeding the cast for the summer, and even paying a couple of leads a small salary; publicity, meaning posters and newspaper ads; costumes and furniture rentals and props; and gas and electric and phone bills. The ticket sales weren't going to cover that. If worst came to worst he'd drop down into Kentucky or North Carolina for a week or two of writing paper, but he hated that kind of thing, and avoided it whenever he possibly could. Passing bum checks was no more illegal than knocking over armored cars, but there was a difference that he found important; a check passer is an actor, he uses an actor's talents and methods, but a heavy heister uses different talents entirely. It bothered Grofield to use his acting abilities that way, it seemed somehow degrading.

But now, looking at his theater in the bright light of the first warm sunny day of spring, Grofield made a bitter face and decided that if he didn't hear from anybody with work by the first of May, he'd have to do the check-writing bit for a few days or a week, in order to bankroll the coming season.

As it was, he was running as tight a ship as he could. Both farmhouses were rented out, and he and Mary were living in the theater, sleeping in a bedroom set laid out on a platform rolled into the wings, using the theater john, Mary cooking their meals on the double hotplate in the girls' dressing room down under the stage. By the middle of June, though, the tenants would have to be kicked out of the nearer farmhouse, the one just across the county road, so the cast would have a place to stay.

So he'd write paper, that's all. In a good week, working through two or three states, he could write fifteen or twenty thousand and have enough to last the summer. Sticking to revivals.

"Revivals," he said aloud. He was disgusted. He shook his head at the empty seats and turned away to go over to where the flats were stored against the rear wall on the side opposite where the door had been rolled back. The flats were in various sizes ranging from three feet wide and eight feet high to five feet wide and twelve feet high, and all were made of muslin attached to a simple frame of one-by-four pine boards. Water-base paint had been used to paint the scenery of last year's shows on the flats, and now they were stacked in no particular order, a jumble of fake walls and doors and windows in different colors and styles and periods.

Grofield began to carry the flats, one by one, over to the opening in the rear wall, and lowered them the six feet to the ground. When he'd moved about ten, he jumped to the ground, carried a flat around to the side of the building, leaned it against the wall, picked up the hose he'd already attached to the faucet out there, and began to hose the flat down.

What he was doing was removing the paint. Muslin is light, but paint is heavy. Any frail girl can carry an unpainted canvas flat, but with three or four coats of paint on it a strong man can barely lift the thing. Grofield, like most thrifty theater operators, removed last year's water-base paint every spring so he could use the old flats again. In addition to the hose, he also had a scrub brush and a ladder, so he could scrub the paint loose after the first hosing. The second hosing usually did the job, though sometimes he had to give a spot or two an extra treatment with the scrub brush and a third stream of water from the hose.

Grofield liked theater work, everything to do with the stage, even simple manual labor like this. He worked along in the bright sun, the soft spring air all around him, the water cold, the paint running down the flats in long streams, and after a while, despite his money troubles, he began to whistle.

2

The car that turned off the blacktop county road into the gravel parking lot beside the theater was a bronze Plymouth with Texas plates. Grofield stood on the ladder with the scrub brush in one hand and the hose in the other and looked at it.

He'd been working an hour now. Seven gray-white flats were lined up along the side wall of the barn, drying; he was working now on the eighth. The ground all around him ran with colors, reds and yellows and whites and blues and greens, all different shades, running together and making new colors, a bright kaleidoscope of color spread out on the ground in colored water, running and flowing every which way through the tough new spring blades of grass. Grofield, too, was varicolored, in his work pants and sneakers and T-shirt, wet and colorful. He stood leaning on the ladder, elbows resting on the top rung, scrub brush in his right hand, hose dribbling in his left, and watched the car angle across the parking lot toward him and finally come to a stop. He waited for the driver to get out and ask directions; what else would this be?

It was Dan Leach. He got out from behind the wheel and called, "Hello, Grofield, what are you doing?"

"Washing flats," Grofield said. "You got good news for me?"

"Could be," Dan said. "Come on down off the ladder, lemme show you something."

Grofield got down off the ladder. "What I want to know is, do you have a job for me. Better than that Myers thing, I mean. Did you ever find him?"

"I'll tell you all about it." Dan looked around. "How private are we here?"

"Nobody can hear us."

"What about seeing us?"

Grofield nodded at the farmhouse across the county road. "There's people home over there."

"You know any place private?"

Grofield looked at him. "What for?"

"I wanna show you something. Come on, let's take a ride."

Grofield looked at his wet hands, down at his wet clothes, back at the flats. "Is this something real, Dan? What's the big secret?"

"I don't want to open the trunk where anybody else can see us," Dan said. "You know me, Grofield, I don't make jokes."

"That's right," Grofield said. "My clothes are a mess, you know. You want me in the car, or should I go change?"

"It ain't my car," Dan said. "It's Myers'."

Grofield brightened. "You found him, eh?"

"Get in. That's what I've got to show you."

Grofield got in, on the passenger's side, and Dan got back behind the wheel. Dan said, "Give me directions."

"Pull out onto the road and turn left," Grofield said.

3

When Dan opened the trunk, Andrew Myers was lying in there, curled up in a ball. Grofield blinked at him, thinking he was dead, but then Myers moved, lifting his head and blinking in the light, looking blind and confused and scared. "What now?" he said. His voice croaked, as though he were very dry.

"Climb out of there," Dan said.

Myers moved his arms and legs feebly. "I can hardly move."

Dan reached in and jabbed him in the side with his thumb a couple of times, just above the belt. "Don't make me wait," he said.

"I'm moving. I'm moving."

Grofield stepped back, and watched Myers painfully lift himself up and start to climb out of the trunk. He said, "How long's he been in there?"

"Since Houston," Dan said. "No, I'm a liar. He was out for twenty minutes yesterday."

Myers was having a tough time, and now Grofield saw why. He was handcuffed, but in a strange way; his left wrist was handcuffed to his left ankle.

Grofield stepped forward to help him get over the lip of the trunk and out onto the ground, but Dan said, "Leave the bastard alone. He'll make it."

Grofield frowned. "Why make it so tough on him?"

"How's the back of your head?" Dan asked him.

Grofield shrugged. "All right. He hit me only once. I'm not that upset any more."

"I am," Dan said.

Grofield looked at him. "You didn't get your cash back?"

"He spent it before I got to him, the son of a bitch." Leach stepped forward suddenly and grabbed Myers by the hair and yanked. "Will you get out of there!" Myers fell out onto the ground.

They were on a dirt road about two miles from the theater, in the woods. Only a few tubes of sunlight angled down through the branches, and it was cooler in here. Grofield's clothes, still wet, were getting chilly and uncomfortable.

Myers rolled around on the dirt until he got his feet under him, and then slowly stood up, his right hand using the car for support. When he was standing, he was bent far down and to the left, the fingers of his left hand touching the ground. His wrist was rubbed raw by the handcuff. When he looked up at Grofield he had to open his mouth wide to be able to lift his head far enough up to meet Grofield's eyes. In that position, he looked feeble-minded.

Dan said, "Myers has a story to tell you. Tell him, bastard."

Myers said, "Can I sit down?" He had to lower his head to talk. "I can't talk in this position."

"Sit, stand, I don't care," Dan said. "Just tell him the story."

Myers eased himself to the ground. Now he could get himself into a more ordinary position, his right leg flat out in front of him, left leg raised, left arm down at his side. He leaned his back against the rear bumper of the Plymouth, looked up at Grofield, and said, "I know where there's over a hundred grand, just waiting to be taken." His voice was improving a little with use, but his expression was still pained.

Grofield glanced at Dan, but Dan was looking down at Myers in grim satisfaction. Grofield gave his attention back to Myers.

Myers said, "Dankworth told me about it. He wanted me to go after it with him."

Grofield said, "Dankworth?"

Dan said, "The boy you let frisk you in Vegas."

Grofield frowned. "The one Myers killed?"

"It was him or me," Myers said. He sounded aggrieved, as though he'd been badly treated by someone he'd been kind to.

"Tell me about that," Grofield said.

Dan said, "Listen to the hundred grand."

"In a minute," Grofield told him. "First I want to hear about the gunfight at the O.K. Corral." To Myers he said, "You and Dankworth were such buddies that he told you about this hundred thousand, and he wanted you to come do the caper with him, but then he turned around and tried to kill you?"

"He lost confidence in me," Myers said, some of the grievance still showing in his voice. "After you people walked out."

"The others left, too?"

Dan said, "Right after us. All three of them."

Grofield said, "Whose idea was it to hijack Dan and me?"

"Mine," Myers said. "I was mad at you people, you

were the first ones to go. Maybe if you didn't leave, the others—"

"If they were pros," Dan said, a little irritated, "they'd have left."

"Anyway," Grofield said. "You and whatsisname—"

"Dankworth."

"I didn't ask you. You and whatsisname came down after everybody left, and you saw Dan and me at the table, and you saw us winning."

"We couldn't get too close," Myers said. "We thought you were the one with the money."

"And you wanted to get even for us walking out on you."

"That's right."

"So then whatsisname—"

"Dankworth."

Dan stepped forward and kicked Myers on the right kneecap. "He didn't ask you!"

Myers didn't make a noise, but he winced and closed his free hand around his knee.

Grofield shook his head at Dan. "I don't like to see people being hurt," he said. To Myers he said, "Dankworth. After you got Dan's money and went back to the hotel room, he jumped you."

"That's right."

"And you had a fight, and you managed to win."

"That's right."

Grofield turned half away from Myers and said to Dan, "If he tells a dumb lie on that part, why should I believe his hundred thousand story?"

Aggrieved again, Myers said, "What do you mean, a dumb lie?"

Dan was frowning. He studied Myers, and then looked at Grofield. "You sound damn sure of yourself."

"I am. Number one—there wasn't any mess in either room, no struggle of any kind. There was some bloodstain on the rug in front of one of the chairs, and that was it. Number two—the only way you can kill a man the way Dankworth was killed is to sneak up behind him when he's sitting down, reach around him, pull his head up by the chin with one hand and slit his throat with your knife in the other hand. You don't give a man that kind of cut from in front of him, and you don't give him that kind of cut if you're in a brawl with him."

Myers said, "Why the hell would I want to kill him?"

Grofield turned back to him. "Because Dan knocked him out, and *you* lost confidence in *him.* You needed him till you worked some sort of scam for ready money, but once you got Dan's thirteen thousand you were through with him. And you were mad at the world anyway, because all the rest of us walked out on you. And you wanted all of Dan's money for yourself."

Myers blinked, his mouth working as he tried to think of something to say. No words came out.

Dan, sounding dangerous, said, "You son of a bitch, is that the way it was?"

Grofield said, "Don't start kicking him, Dan. I just wanted to get that part straight before I heard about the hundred thousand." He looked at Myers. "I'll listen now."

Myers wanted to turn sullen, but was afraid to. He said, "This is for real. I don't have any reason to lie about this."

"Just tell it," Grofield suggested.

"All right." Myers wiped his mouth with the back of his free hand, and put the hand back on his hurt knee. He said, "Dankworth was in prison up till the beginning of this year."

"Doesn't surprise me," said Grofield.

"This was near Los Angeles," Myers said, "in a state penitentiary there. He got to know an old man there, named Entrekin, they were friends, I suppose. And it turned out this Entrekin and two other old men, all of them long-term prisoners, they had a tunnel to the outside. Dankworth got out through it, that's how he made his escape, this is all absolutely on the level. He's still listed in California as an escaped felon, you can look it up."

"I don't want to look it up," Grofield said. "I'll accept the fact that Dankworth was an escaped con, and that he got out through somebody else's tunnel. Proceed."

"All right," Myers said. "Now, the point about these three old men and their tunnel is that they don't want to get out of prison! Do you see? They're all old. They don't want to spend the last years of their lives hiding out from the police. They don't care about women any more. So the way it seems to them, they're better off if they stay behind bars."

Grofield glanced again at Dan, but Dan was watching Myers.

Myers said, "But they've all got families, all three of them, wives and children and grandchildren and everything, all on the outside. And they want to take care of their families, naturally, so what they do is, they go out at night and they do burglaries all around Los Angeles. Two or three nights a week they go out and they do these little burglaries, what Dankworth called stings. They do three or four stings a night, every night they go out, up and down the California coast around Los Angeles, and they never take anything except cash. And they have a little studio apartment somewhere near the Sunset Strip, where they keep the money. And they send money to their families that way."

Grofield smiled. "That's a very nice story," he said. "I really hope it's true, because it's so nice. They're taking care of their families."

"That's exactly right," Myers said.

Dan said, "The sweet thing is, you can't have a better alibi than them. They can't be pulling any of these jobs, they're in stir."

"It's a nice story," Grofield said. He was still smiling, the story had made him happy.

Myers said, "There's more to it than that. It seems they've been saving money up, not turning it all over to their families, because they want to leave them something really good when they die. To have an estate, you see."

"An estate," Grofield repeated. He was grinning broadly. "I like those three guys."

"Well," Myers said, "Entrekin told Dankworth they had over a hundred thousand dollars stashed in their apartment, and this was last year. It has to be even more by now."

"That troubles me," Grofield said. "Why would this smart old man tell Dankworth so much?"

"I guess he liked him," Myers said. "And of course, Dankworth was supposed to be there for a minimum of twelve more years, even if he got a parole at the earliest possible moment. He didn't want to tell Dankworth exactly where the tunnel was, and Dankworth had to force it out of him. So he could escape."

"Misplaced confidence," Grofield said. "It runs the world. The old man trusted Dankworth. Dankworth trusted you. And now we're supposed to trust you."

"No trust involved at all," Dan said. "Wait him out, and then I'll tell you my idea."

"I'm still listening," Grofield said.

Myers said, "The old man wouldn't tell Dankworth where the apartment was, not exactly. He mentioned once that it was near the Sunset Strip, but that was all. But the thing is, there's over a hundred thousand dollars hidden there—in cash! And Dankworth told me exactly where the tunnel comes out on the outside of the prison."

"That was a mistake, wasn't it?" Grofield said. "If he'd held that back, he'd be alive now."

Dan said, "That's neither here nor there. The point is, a guy could keep an eye on that tunnel until the three of them come out, and then follow them. They might go do their stings first, but sooner or later they'd wind up at the apartment. Then you'd wait until they left to go back to the pen, and you'd break in, find the cash, and take off."

Grofield made a face. "I hate taking their money," he said. "I like them too much."

"You don't have to take it," Dan said. "I'll take it. This is a one-man job."

Frowning at him, Grofield said, "Then what do you want me for?"

"My big question is," said Dan, "what do I do with this bastard? I can't carry him around with me until I do the job, he'd be in the way and screw things up. I've gotta stash him somewhere until the job's over, so just in case it's all bullshit I can come back and make him pay for it."

Grofield shook his head. "Not with me," he said. "If that's what you have in mind, I'm sorry."

Dan said, "How long could it be for? A week? And you've got plenty of room to stash him. In that theater of yours."

"No," Grofield said. "I don't bring my work home."

"I'll give ten percent of whatever I find," Dan said. "If he's telling the truth, it's better than ten grand for you."

Grofield felt the temptation, but shook his head again and said, "I'm sorry, Dan, but I just won't do it. I won't risk losing what I've got here. And besides that, I won't put my wife in a potentially dangerous situation, which is what this is."

Dan said, irritably, "What the hell am I gonna do with him?"

Grofield shrugged. "You got your money's worth out of him. Let him go. He won't louse up your play in Los Angeles."

"That's right," Myers said eagerly.

"See that? He isn't that anxious to see you again. Let him run home to Texas."

Dan grimaced, not liking it. "But what if he's lying? Sends me out on some half-ass stunt, watching an alley where a tunnel's supposed to come out—what if there isn't any tunnel, and he's making a damn fool of me?"

"You found him before, you could find him again."

"I don't wanna let him off that easy," Dan said angrily, and he looked for a second as though he was going to start kicking Myers again.

Grofield said, "Then kill him. Not around here, take him—"

"Hey!" Myers said, and stared at Grofield as though he'd been betrayed.

Dan said, "I don't wanna kill anybody, that's not where I'm at. I *steal*."

"Well, it's one or the other," Grofield said. "Stashing him with me or anybody else is a bad idea. What if he gets loose while you're gone, kills me and Mary, and when you come back he's laying for you?"

"You'd watch him better than that."

"Would I? Forget it, Dan. Kill him or let him go. Believe him about these old men and their tunnel or don't believe him."

"I'll have to think about it," Dan said grumpily.

Grofield said, "Would you drive me back? I'm getting cold in these wet clothes."

"Sure." Dan nudged Myers with his foot. "Back in the trunk."

"Let me sit in the back seat," Myers said. There was a whine in his voice now. "I won't do anything, just let me sit in the back seat."

"The only reason I'm not hitting you right now," Dan told him, "is because my friend doesn't like to watch that kind of thing. But don't give me a lot of aggravation to remember later on, when he's gone, or I'll make you very unhappy. Now get back in the trunk."

Myers struggled up again, and back into the trunk. Grofield wanted to go sit in the car, but he thought he should stick around and watch until Myers was tucked away. Dan might start punching and kicking out of irritation and frustration.

Finally Myers was in, lying on his side in that cramped

fetal-like position, and Dan slammed the lid again. "Come on, I'll take you home."

They got in the car, and Grofield gave directions, and they started up.

Driving, Dan said, "I don't know what to do."

"Let him go," Grofield said. "The aggravation isn't worth it."

"I'll have to think about it."

4

Mary called, "Dinner!"

Grofield was on the platform containing the bedroom set, changing his clothes again. When Dan had dropped him off, he'd changed out of the wet stuff into different work clothes, and had gone back to washing flats, which meant he'd immediately gotten all wet again. But he didn't mind it so much when he was moving around and in sunlight. He'd gotten most of them finished by the time Mary came home from her job at the supermarket, her arms full of groceries, some of which she'd paid for, and he'd gone ahead and done the last two flats before coming in to clean up and change. The sun was going down, it was getting chillier, and he was just as glad to switch again to dry clothes.

The bedroom set had two walls, made of flats, with the double bed against one and the mirrored dresser against the other. An armless wooden kitchen chair stood out in limbo at the wall-less corner of the platform, and mismatched end tables with mismatched bedside lamps flanked the bed, completing the furnishings. Extension cords ran from the lamps back into the wings and plugged in at the lightboard.

Dressed again, Grofield stepped down from the platform and crossed from stage left to stage right. The central part of the stage, the main playing area, was done as a living room, but only with the furniture, without any flats to give the illusion of walls and doors and windows, so that behind the furniture there was only space, filled with odd pieces of stage junk, and then the rear wall of the barn. As for the living room set, a wide, low maroon mohair sofa was exactly in the middle of the stage, facing the audience, on an old faded imitation Persian rug. End tables flanked it, with a table lamp on the left and a floor lamp on the right. A black leather chair, sideways to the audience, was stage left of the sofa. A lone bookcase, eight feet high and three feet wide, stood in naked solitude about six feet back from the black leather chair. Stage right of the sofa, set back a ways, was a rocking chair, and beside it a drum table holding a fake telephone.

Grofield crossed now behind all this furniture, and stepped up on a platform on the other side that contained a dining room set. Two walls again, one with a window that looked out on the rear wall of the barn. An old but sturdy maple dining room table and four chairs, two of them matching the table and the other two odd strays. A maple bureau from some forgotten bedroom suite was standing against the windowless wall; it was in the drawers of this bureau that Mary kept their dishes and silverware and tablecloths.

And candles. Two were burning on the table now, which Mary had already set. She wasn't in sight, and as Grofield stepped up on the platform the stage lights dimmed, lowering till the candlelight became obvious on the table. Grofield bent and peered past a side drapery backstage; Mary was at the lightboard, just releasing the master lever. "Be right there," she called, and waved to him, and went off to the star's dressing room to get dinner off the hotplates.

Grofield sat down at his place. He was facing the audience now. The house lights were out, so all he could see was the darkness out there beyond the living room set. It was a comforting darkness, somehow, warm and pleasant, and he smiled at it. This hopeless theater was more home than anyplace else he'd ever lived.

Mary came out with dinner; meat loaf and one vegetable, broccoli from the supermarket freezer. She was on the small side, neat and compact, and looked like the heroine of a thirties musical. Grofield was out of his mind for her.

While Grofield served meat loaf and broccoli onto their plates, she went off again, this time to the refrigerator in the green room, and brought back a half-bottle of moselle; at a dollar per half bottle, it was one luxury they could go on affording.

During dinner, she said, "Who was it came to see you today? Anybody I should know about?" She knew about his other career, he'd met her in the course of a robbery four years ago, but they didn't often go into the details together.

Grofield swallowed meat loaf and said, "How do you know somebody came to see me?"

"Mrs. Brady told me." That was the tenant in the farmhouse across the road. "She said you went for a ride with him. In a Plymouth. And it was from Texas."

Grofield grinned, shaking his head. "The smaller the community, the tougher it is to have any privacy. It was Dan Leach, the fellow that won the money when I was in Las Vegas. I told you about that, remember?"

"Did he have a job for you?" She looked eager; she knew their financial condition.

"Not exactly." He told her about the afternoon and Myers, and the three old prisoners with their tunnel and their hundred thousand dollars.

"It doesn't seem right to take their money," Mary said. "I'm glad you said no."

"I know what you mean, but that wasn't why I said no."

She went on, following her own line of thought, saying, "What you do is best. Taking from banks and armored cars and places like that. That's not really *stealing,* because you aren't taking from people, you're taking from institutions. Institutions don't count. They *ought* to support us."

Grofield grinned at her. "You'll make a great defense witness."

She made a face. "Don't joke about that."

After dinner they did the dishes together, and then Grofield turned on the radio. It was tuned permanently to a background music station that played lots of Mantovani and nothing recorded later than 1955, and it was hooked in to the theater's speaker system. With the volume fairly low, the theater was filled with lush music, which seemed to drift gently down from the raftered cathedral-type ceiling like spring rain.

They sat together on the sofa, facing the empty seats out there in the darkness, and talked, mostly about the plays they might do this coming season. Later on, they made love on the sofa, and fell asleep there, wrapped around each other.

5

He heard a sound.

Grofield opened his eyes, seeing nothing but Mary's rumpled black hair, and for a second or two he couldn't figure out where he was—face down, entangled, warm all over except for his backside.

He lifted his head, and Mary made a small grumbling noise in her throat and moved her head slightly from left to right. He looked down at her sleeping face, listening. He looked up, looked around the dim-lit stage, the dark body of the theater.

There was someone there. He couldn't see anybody, he couldn't really even hear anything, he didn't know precisely where the someone was, but he knew he and Mary were no longer alone.

A small shiver started in the base of his spine, where his bare skin was cold anyway, and ran lightly up his backbone like mercury through a thermometer. He and Mary were in the light, however dim, both of them half naked. The intruder was in darkness.

Mary was frowning in her sleep. She moved her head again, disturbed by the tension in Grofield's body. Resting his weight on his right elbow, jammed down between her shoulder and the sofa back, he slowly moved up his left hand and cupped it over her mouth.

Her eyes opened, startled. He felt her mouth strain against his palm, wanting to yell. He stared tensely down at her, and slowly shook his head back and forth. The fright faded from her eyes, and she nodded. He released her mouth leaned on both elbows, and lowered his head beside hers to whisper in her ear, "There's someone in the theater. Out in the seats someplace."

She whispered, "What are you going to do?"

"I'm heading for the lightboard. You stay here. Don't move unless I yell at you to."

"All right. Do you think it's that man Myers?"

That hadn't occurred to Grofield. He'd thought of it as a peeping tom, maybe some local high school boy. But if Dan had taken Grofield's advice and released Myers, and if he'd done it too close to here, it was just possible that Myers would show up. Myers was very unprofessional, which meant unpredictable, there was no telling what his response might be to anything.

"Let's hope it isn't," Grofield said. "I'm going now."

"All right."

Grofield tensed himself, bringing his knees up slightly underneath him to get more leverage, then abruptly pushed himself upward with hands and knees and rolled violently to the right, over the top of the sofa and onto the dusty thin carpet behind it. He landed heavily on his left side, having turned almost completely around, rolled onto his stomach, got his feet under him, and made a fast weaving dash, bent double, to the wings and the lightboard, where he simultaneously pushed the stage lighting master lever all the way down and the house lights lever all the way up.

It was a quick step to the left to look out past the edge of the opened curtain at the house. The stage seemed just as bright as ever, with spill from the house lights, and poor Mary was lying there on the sofa unmoving, in the traditional pose of the naked woman trying to cover herself.

And there was no one to be seen in the house. The seats stretched back, level after level, absolutely empty. The four entrance doors at the rear were all closed.

Had he been wrong? But he had a sense for that kind of thing, he'd come by it naturally and he'd trained it in the service of his other profession. He'd heard some sort of sound, something small but real, which had awakened him and told him there was another presence somewhere nearby. Not a cat, not a squirrel, both of which made occasional visits. Something human.

There was a tool kit up on top of the lightboard. Grofield reached into it, came out with a ballpeen hammer, and turned it so the ball was the business end. He felt stupid, dressed in nothing but a polo shirt, but his trousers and shoes and everything else were over on the floor in front of the sofa. There was neither time nor opportunity to dress.

Grofield ducked out from behind the curtain, made the edge of the stage in two running steps, and jumped down. He trotted up the center aisle, going up a level at every second step, and scanned to left and right as he ran. The hammer was ready in his right hand.

And there was nobody there. He stood at the top finally, up by the doors, and looked around, and he was absolutely alone. He glanced back at Mary, who had moved nothing but her head, so she could watch him, and he was about to call to her that it was a false alarm when he heard the thud.

From where? He cocked an ear and listened, and it happened again, a dull-sounding thud, muffled, from behind him.

From the doors.

He turned around and frowned at the doors. The other side of them was a large square platform built out from the face of the barn, ten feet above the ground, to match the height of the rear rows of seats inside. Wide wooden steps led down to ground level, with wood railings up the sides of the steps and around the platform.

There was someone—or something—out on the platform. The thud came again, sounding very low on the end door to the left, and Grofield frowned again, trying to figure out what it was. It wasn't the rapping sound of knuckles, but it wasn't the scratching noise a cat or a dog makes either.

Feeling more foolish and vulnerable than ever with no clothes on—and with this hammer in his hand—Grofield went down to the last door at the other end from the noise, slowly and silently unlocked it, and abruptly pushed it open and jumped out into nighttime darkness.

There was a quarter moon, and a sky full of stars, giving just a little light. Enough to see the shape of a body lying face down on the boards of the platform over to the left. As Grofield watched, the body pushed itself slowly up on its elbows, and lunged forward, thudding its head into the door.

Grofield peered around, but saw no one else. Cautiously he approached the body, which had collapsed again after hitting the door. Was it familiar?

Dan Leach.

"Good Christ," Grofield whispered. Still staring down at Dan, he backed up to the open doorway and called, "Get your clothes on and bring me my pants. It's somebody hurt."

6

Mary called, "Hey!"

Grofield was on the roof in the sunlight, with shingles and nails and a hammer. He looked down. "What?"

"He's awake."

"Delirious?"

"No, really awake this time. He wants to talk to you."

"I just get started on something—" Grofield grumbled, and shook his head. "I'll be right there. Soon as I finish this one I started."

She was keeping the sun from her eyes with one hand, and now she waved the other and moved off, disappearing from his sight when she approached the building.

It was two days since they'd brought Dan in, bleeding from four knife wounds, and put him to bed on an Army cot in the men's dressing room. Mary, afraid he'd die, had wanted to call the First Aid Squad ambulance to take him to the hospital, but Grofield had known that would be bad for everybody and had insisted they could nurse Dan themselves. Mary had gotten the first aid book from the box-office down at ground level under the rear theater seats and they'd followed its instruction. And apparently it was working out.

Grofield finished with the shingle he'd been putting in, hooked the hammer over a nail partway driven into the roof, made sure the rest of the new shingles and the bag of nails weren't going to slide off, and then made his way down the slanting roof to the ladder, and then to the ground.

Dan looked very pale, but he was awake. He said, "You got a beautiful wife."

Mary looked pleased. Grofield said, "And you've only got eight more lives."

"How'd you know where to find me?"

"You came knocking at the door. Don't you remember?"

Dan frowned. "Are you putting me on?"

"No. You came here and crawled up the steps out front and beat your head against the door till we let you in. Don't you remember any of it?"

"The last thing I remember is Myers with that knife."

"Where the hell did he get a knife?"

"From the car. It was his car, you know, he had one in a sheath under the dash. I left it there, I didn't need any knife."

There was a folding chair closed up and leaning against the wall. Grofield opened it and sat down. "Tell me what happened," he said. "From the beginning."

"I took your goddam advice," Dan said. "That's what happened."

"You let him go."

"I underestimate the bastard. I do it every time. I took him back to where I had him tell you the story, and I let him go there."

"Thanks a lot. You couldn't take him a few hundred miles first."

"I was sore," Dan said. "I just wanted to get rid of him."

"Not around me."

"You're right. I wasn't thinking. Anyway, he didn't come here."

"That's lucky for you, he might have finished the job. Will you tell me what happened?"

"I got him out of the trunk, and took off the cuffs, and he got a lucky kick in at my head. He got me down and hit me with a rock, and I was out for a few seconds or a minute or something, and when I was getting up he came back around the car with the knife and let me have it. I thought I was dead."

"And that's it?"

"Till I opened my eyes and saw your wife. It beats me how I got here."

"It beats me," Grofield said, "that you weren't seen."

Dan reached up a shaky hand and wiped his mouth. He was still very weak; the talking had worn him, and he was beginning to breathe hard. He said, "Can I stay? I know how you feel about—" He let the sentence lapse.

Grofield shook his head. "There's no choice," he said. "Naturally you'll stay."

"Only for a few days, till I get my strength back."

It would be more than that, but Grofield didn't say so. "Sure," he said, and got to his feet. "Your wallet looked pretty fat when I undressed you. I'll want you to pay your way."

"Sure," Dan said. "Take what you want."

"Just your expenses," Grofield said. "Ordinarily I wouldn't, but we're running kind of tight."

Mary said, "Do you like minestrone? Canned, I mean."

"Sure."

"Rest for a while," she said, "and I'll make it. Come on, Alan, let him rest."

They went out and shut the door, and Grofield said, "I'm sorry about this."

"That's all right. We'll say he's my cousin that came to visit and caught a cold on the trip and has to stay in bed for a while."

Grofield grinned at her. "Okay."

7

When the phone started to ring, Grofield was on the ladder, a paint brush in his hand. He was putting a new coat of white on the words MEAD GROVE THEATER that filled the whole side of the barn facing the country road.

"Crap," he said. Mary was at work, he'd have to answer it himself. He put the brush in the bucket standing on the ladder top, and went hurriedly down to the ground.

He was now about midway between the two phones, one extension in the box-office to his right and one backstage near the lightboard. He hesitated, while the phone started a third ring, and then trotted around to the big open doorway leading to the stage. He went up the wooden ladder fixed to the outer wall and headed across the stage. Dan was sitting on the leather chair in the living room set, crossways to the house so he could get a little sun from the open door. This was the first day he was up and around, after being here a week. He looked pale and thin, but itchy and impatient. He lifted a hand in a slow weak wave as Grofield trotted by at an angle toward the lightboard.

"Hello?"

"Grofield?" The voice was male, heavy, somewhat indistinct.

"Speaking."

"This is Barnes."

The name had a familiar sound to it, but Grofield made no immediate connections. He said, "Barnes?"

"From Salt Lake City."

"Oh!" Now he remembered, and an image of Ed Barnes flashed in his mind—a tall man, very broad in the shoulder but somewhat gone to fat, about forty years old, with thin black hair and a lumpy formless nose. Grofield had worked with Barnes once, on a bank job in Salt Lake City.

Barnes was saying, "You free?"

"As a bird," Grofield said.

"Could you get to St. Louis tomorrow?"

"Yes."

"Meet Charles Martin at the Hotel Hoyle."

"Done."

Grofield hung up and went back across the stage toward Dan. "I'm leaving tomorrow for a while," he said.

Dan looked sour. "You got something?"

"You know Ed Barnes?"

"I worked with him once or twice."

"If it works out," Grofield said, "you'll probably be gone before I get back."

"Could they use another man?"

"Dan, you aren't ready."

"I know it, goddam it." Dan glowered toward the wings. "When I get my hands on that son of a bitch—"

"Be sure you're ready first," Grofield said.

"I'll be ready."

Grofield nodded, and said, "I'm going back to work." He walked over to the doorway and was about to jump down when Dan called his name. Dan's voice was all right until he tried to shout, and then it thinned out.

Grofield looked back, and Dan called, "Thanks."

"Sure," Grofield said, and jumped to the ground, and walked back around to finish painting the letters.

St. Louis

I

Grofield wrote *Charles Martin* on the registration card, and pushed it across to the desk clerk.

"Yes, Mr. Martin. And you'll be staying with us how long?"

"I'm not sure yet. A day or two."

"Yes, sir. That will be room four-twelve."

"Are there any messages for me?"

"One moment, I'll check."

The clerk rippled through an uneven stack of envelopes. "Yes, sir, just the one."

Grofield took the envelope. "Thank you."

"Front!"

The bellboy took Grofield's suitcase. Grofield put the envelope away in his inside jacket pocket, and followed the bellboy to the elevator. The Hotel Hoyle was old, and old fashioned, in a downtown section of St. Louis that hadn't been fashionable since before World War I. It was now a competent commercial travelers' hotel, and the lobby carpeting had paths worn in it, like rabbit trails in the woods.

The elevator was self-service, a nice combination of modernization and economy. The bellboy, a skinny black youth who looked as though he lived on a diet of bones, pushed 4, and the elevator rose slowly upward in its shaft. Grofield could hear the clicking of the descent guards all the way up.

The room was small but functional, dominated by a wide old-fashioned window that overlooked a blacktop parking lot and the many-faceted face of an office building. Grofield gave the bellboy a dollar, double-locked the door after him, and opened his envelope.

Wood's Bar, East St. Louis, Eleven P.M.

2

St. Louis, on the Missouri side of the Mississippi River, is a city, like any other. East St. Louis, across the bridge on the Illinois side, is the city's underbelly. Here are the late-night bars, the cruising hookers, everything you can't find in the Yellow Pages. The streets are dark, the neon seems undernourished, and the soldiers and airmen from the bases around the city keep the money supply fat and moving.

Grofield sat at the bar in the long blue-gray room called Wood's Bar, and nursed a bottle of Budweiser—support local business. On a narrow stage up behind the backbar a tired and aging mixed-race jazz quintet tried to figure out how to make the transition to rock. So far, all they were sure of was the volume level; you couldn't hear yourself think. Looking at the conversations going on up and down the bar, and in the booths behind him, Grofield decided the place must be full of lip readers.

He'd gotten here five minutes early, and now it was five minutes late. Where the hell was Barnes?

A hand touched his shoulder. He turned his head, and Barnes nodded at him and went toward the door. Grofield considered finishing his beer, but it had no head left at all by now, so he left it, got off the stool and followed Barnes out to the street.

"Glad you could make it," Barnes said, and pointed to a Pontiac parked across the way. In this light, it looked black, but it probably wasn't.

They went across the street, and Grofield waited on the curb while Barnes unlocked the driver's door, got in, and reached across to unlock the door on Grofield's side. Grofield slid in and said, "I hope this one works out. I went out on a dud about a month ago."

"You're gonna like this," Barnes said. "Simple, fast, and fat."

"You just described my ideal."

Barnes drove a dozen blocks and turned in at the shut door of a parking garage closed for the night. "Go give a triple knock on the door," he said.

"Right."

Grofield went out and knocked, and a second later the door slid up. The inside was a big square, low-ceilinged, concrete-floored, half full of parked cars. An office with windows all the way around was in the middle; the only light was in there, a fluorescent fixture hanging from the ceiling.

Barnes drove in, Grofield walked in beside him, and the door slid down again. Barnes steered the Pontiac on over to the office, and Grofield walked after him, getting there as Barnes was climbing out of the car. "They're in here."

Two of them; Grofield didn't know either one. One was sitting on the chair beside the filing cabinet, the other was standing beside the small littered desk.

Barnes made the introduction—"Alan Grofield. Steve Tebelman. Fred Hughes."

They all nodded at one another. Steve Tebelman was the one sitting in the chair. He was dressed in a somewhat shabby dark suit, as though he'd come out for a job interview and really needed the job. Fred Hughes was the one standing by the desk, and he was in dark green workshirt and matching pants, with *Hughes* in yellow script lettering sewn above the shirt pocket.

Barnes nodded at Hughes. "Fred's our set-up man."

Grofield raised an eyebrow. "It's a local job?"

"Belleville," Hughes said. "About twelve miles east of here."

Grofield looked at Barnes. "That isn't usual," he reminded him. Usually the organizational meetings before a job took place in some other part of the country from where the heist would be. It was better to spend as little time in the neighborhood of a robbery beforehand as possible.

"I know," Barnes said. "But I told you, this one's fast. Fred's a pro, he knows what he's doing."

"It's already cased," Hughes said.

Grofield didn't say anything. He looked at Hughes, thinking about it. He could be a professional, but how good could he be and have a job parking cars? And how good could he be and want to pull a caper in his own neighborhood?

Hughes said, "I know what you're thinking. I been here six months is all. I belong in Florida, and I'll go there a couple months from now."

Grofield said, "Not right after we pull this."

Hughes had a very dry thin way of smiling. "No," he said. "I've had a run of second-best hands. I know I don't look my best right now, but I'm not a busher."

The other one, Steve Tebelman, said, "Let's get down to it." He was about the same age as Hughes, early thirties, and something about his dry brown hair and the crumpled cigarette he was smoking made Grofield think he was a hillbilly, out of Tennessee or Kentucky or someplace like that. And out of prison not too long ago, that too.

"That's a good idea," Barnes said. "I already know about it. Fred, tell Steve and Alan."

"Right." Hughes leaned back against the desk and folded his arms. "They got an Air Force base out there, called Scott. They get paid twice a month, the last day of the month and the fifteenth. By check. So the whole town is full of money twice a month."

Barnes said, "This is a big air base they got out there, it covers miles. It's like a training base, with all kinds of schools."

Grofield nodded, listening.

Hughes said, "There's a Food King Supermarket out on the highway near where the married guys live with their families."

"Food King?"

"Like A&P," Barnes said. "It's a chain out around here."

"A lot of the Air Force wives," Hughes said, "they cash their husbands' paychecks there twice a month, when they buy the groceries. So what Food King does, the second and last weeks of the month they don't make any deposits in the bank. All the cash they get in they keep, because they need so much cash on payday."

Grofield asked, "They've got a safe on the premises?"

"Right. Five years ago three guys from the air base tried to get into the place late at night and blow the safe. They never got near it. Once the store closes down for the night, you use any method you want to get in there, and two things happen. First, a light flashes down at the Belleville police station, and you've got local and state cops all over your back. Second, a siren lets loose, and the Air Police on guard duty at the gate across the highway come over to see what's what."

Barnes said, "And besides that, a county sheriff's car drives into the parking lot and back out again every half hour from eleven at night till seven in the morning."

Grofield grinned. "So far, it doesn't sound very easy."

"Depends how you do it," Hughes said, "and how much you know about the set-up."

Grofield said, "Where's your knowledge come from?"

"I went with a woman down in Florida that came from here. She was a cashier at Food King till they found some rolls of quarters in her bra. She was sore at them for giving her the boot, and she told me their whole layout, even gave me a map."

Grofield said, "What's the likelihood of the cops getting to her after we pull this? They'll check out past employees, they always do."

"They probably won't find her. Last I heard, she was going to New York. The type of woman she was, she could be anywhere by now. And even if they do, they won't get from her to me. We went together only about a month, and she's had herself a pretty active life, and I wasn't using any name then I plan to use again."

"The background she gave you," Grofield said, "are you sure it's still current?"

"As sure as you can be from just going to the store and buying some eggs and taking a look around. They're real pleased with their burglar alarm system, there's no reason they'll want to change it."

"What about the safe?"

"We got to figure they still got the same one," Hughes

said. "She described it to me and I described it to Ed, and he knows what it is."

"An old Mosler," Barnes said. "Six feet high, four feet wide, four feet deep. It's free-standing, but they've built plasterboard walls around it, like it was built in. It's the kind you can peel with no trouble, start at the top corner above the lock and peel it like a Polaroid print. Those three Air Force guys were amateurs, it isn't the kind of safe you want to blow at all."

"The only problem," Hughes said, "is that it's in the front of the store, facing the windows. See, across the front are the cash registers, starting at the left, where the store entrance is, and going most of the way across. Then there's the manager's office, that's built up on a platform. When you're up in there the walls are maybe shoulder height. You know, so the manager can look out and see the store all the time."

"I've seen that kind of set-up," Grofield said.

"Yeah, but here's the difference. Most places like that, the safe is pretty small, and it's right up there in the manager's office. But this place, because they keep so much cash around all the time, they have to have this big monster, and I guess they were worried about the weight up on the platform or something. So it's down at floor level, between the manager's office and the side wall. The office and the safe are set back about five feet from the windows, the same as the check-out counters, and there's a waist-high wrought-iron railing across from the window to the corner of the manager's office, to keep the customers out of there. And there's a door on that side of the manager's office, and steps down, so they can go straight from the office to the safe, which is facing the windows."

Grofield said, "So that anybody working on the safe can be seen from outside."

Hughes nodded. "From the parking lot, right."

Grofield said, "So a guy with binoculars should be able to pick up the combination."

"Sorry," Hughes said, and grinned. "They're onto that. They always crowd the safe close when they open it, shield the lock with their body."

"It can be peeled like that anyway," Barnes said, and snapped his fingers.

"Right there by the window," Grofield said.

Steve Tebelman, who'd been very quiet up till now, said, "I'll tell you the truth, I need the money. I keep hoping you're going to tell me how it's going to be easy and safe, and you keep making it sound worse and worse."

Hughes grinned at him. "Don't worry, Steve," he said. "I didn't ask you to come here just for the hell of it."

Grofield said, "You've got it worked out, have you? What to do about the windows?"

"Right," Hughes said. In a quiet way, he was proud of himself.

"And about the burglar alarm?"

"Definitely."

Steve Tebelman said, "The fifteenth is a week from today, next Tuesday. Is that when you want to do it? I mean the night before, Monday?"

Hughes shook his head. "That's when they're the most alert," he said. "They've got the maximum cash in there. The next day, around noon, an armored car comes out from a bank in Belleville with however much more cash they need, but that's never a hell of a lot, not in comparison."

"With what?" Grofield asked. "How much are we talking about?"

"Anywhere between forty and seventy-five thousand."

Tebelman smiled. "That's nice," he said.

Grofield said, "But when do you want to do it?"

"This Friday," Hughes said. "We'll lose two days take, Saturday and Monday, but Friday's the big shopping day anyway, so we'll still make out. And there's other reasons."

"Because of your plan," Grofield suggested.

"Right."

"I can hardly wait to hear it," Grofield said.

3

Grofield stopped at the baby food, and put a dozen jars in his carriage. It was early Wednesday afternoon, the day after the meeting in the garage, and the Food King was barely sprinkled with customers. Grofield walked on, pushing the carriage. He added a carton of corn flakes and turned the corner.

To his right was the row of check-out counters, most of them empty now, only three green-jacketed cashiers on duty, one at the express lane and the other two at the next two counters. Ahead of him, at the end of the check-out counters, were the head-high white partitions of the manager's office. A stocky, worried-looking man could be seen in there, up at a higher level, so he was visible from the shoulders up. He was looking at lists on a clipboard with a younger man in a white shirt and black bow tie.

The white partition of the office ran on to form a corner with the side of the building. Grofield went on down there; racks of pretzels and potato chips were in the corner, and he stood considering them a while. Considering, also, that the rear of the safe was just the other side of those racks. A plywood roof had been put over the safe and a large advertising display for Food King canned fruits and vegetables was standing on top of it.

Grofield finally selected a bag of potato chips, put them in the basket, and moved on. He roamed around the store a few minutes more, then left the carriage up by the meat counter, at the other end of the store from the check-out counters. He went by the dairy case, picked up a couple of vanilla yogurts, paid for them at the express check-out, and went outside to sunshine and the nearly empty parking lot.

In sunlight, Barnes' Pontiac was a medium blue, and dusty. Grofield slid in beside Barnes and looked through the windshield at the store. Specials were advertised in the windows with fat red or blue lettering on large sheets of white paper. Between two of them, Grofield could see the door of the safe in the right front corner, a dark metallic green, about five feet back from the window farthest to the right.

Barnes said, "Like Hughes said?"

"Seems that way. Of course, I don't know about Friday night, if they've still got the same pattern."

"They do," Barnes said, sure of himself. "Every supermarket in the country has that pattern. Friday's the big day, it empties the shelves."

Grofield nodded. "It looks good."

"Seen enough?"

"Sure."

Barnes started the Pontiac and made a looping *U*-turn to take them out to the highway. One of the entrances to Scott Air Force Base was across the highway and about a hundred yards to the right. Automobiles made a more or less steady stream in and out of the place.

Traffic westward on the highway was moderate. Grofield shook one of the vanilla yogurts, to liquefy it, and then drank it from the carton. He offered Barnes the other one, but he didn't want it, so Grofield drank that one down, too, and then said, "If you see a pay phone, stop for me, okay?"

"Sure."

They were all the way in to East St. Louis before Barnes spotted a phone booth and pulled to the curb. Grofield got out, dropped the paper bag with the empty yogurt cartons into a litter basket beside the phone booth, stepped into the booth, and dialed the operator.

"I'd like to make a collect call to the Mead Grove Theater, Mead Grove, Indiana. My name is Grofield."

"One moment, please."

Grofield waited, heard a lot of clicks and buzzes, heard Mary's voice, heard the operator go through the accept-the-charges-ritual and Mary say sure, and then he said, "Honey?"

"Hi! How are you?"

"Fine. I should be back by the middle of next week."

"It that good or bad?"

"I think it's good. Guess who I ran into? Charley Martin. He's staying at the Hotel Hoyle."

"Haven't seen him for a long time," she said. She loved this sort of thing, it made her think of foreign intrigue.

Grofield said, "How's your cousin?"

"Getting better. He's taking a nap now."

"Tell him I asked for him."

"He's really impatient. He's getting mad at himself, he's in such a hurry to be well."

Grofield grinned. "Work him," he said. "Let him rewire the lightboard, that'll take his mind off his troubles."

"Sure it will."

"See you, honey."

"See you. Good luck."

"You bet," Grofield said.

Grofield left the phone booth and got back into the

car, and Barnes drove off, saying, "You're very neat."

"It's a habit. Comes in handy sometimes."

"I can always tell when a man's on the phone with his wife," Barnes said. "The way his face relaxes."

Grofield looked at him in surprise; it wasn't the kind of observation he'd come to expect from a heavy like Barnes. He said, "You married?"

"Not at the moment," Barnes said. He said it flat, and he kept looking out the windshield at the traffic, and Grofield didn't pursue the subject.

4

Route 3 drops south through Illinois, ricocheting from time to time off the Mississippi River, cutting through little towns called Red Bud and Chester and Wolf Lake and Ware. Grofield, sitting beside Hughes in the pale gray Javelin, noticed that the red speedometer needle always pointed exactly at the posted speed limit. Along with setting this job up, Hughes would be their driver, and from all indications he would be a good one.

The car, for one thing. American Motors had done its part for the nation's fantasy life by putting out a car that looked like a Ronson lighter and had more cute tricks than a Boy Scout knife, for children everywhere who liked to play James Bond on the way to work; but they hadn't put much under the hood. They'd called this car Javelin, maybe because you could throw it about as fast as you could drive it. Fred Hughes had taken this car, which had a certain comicbook handsomeness, and had done something to it. The big cat that purred under the hood hadn't come from Kenosha, Wisconsin, not without modifications. The brakes, the shocks, everything about the car felt different from anything that had ever rolled off any assembly line anywhere. Now the car was sleek and powerful and perfectly under control, and Hughes drove it as though it were part of himself—as though it were a prosthetic device attached to his fingertips. Grofield, watching him in silent admiration, felt that

Hughes could make the car do what he wanted simply by looking at it and raising an eyebrow.

The best driver for anything, including going quickly away from where you no longer want to be, is not the guy who will kick the car across the state, the guy who loves speed—the best driver is the guy who loves cars. He'll get more out of the car, and he'll live longer.

They did very little talking together on the drive south. Hughes at one point told him about the financing. "I'm doing it on two grand. That's probably cutting it close, but I don't want to waste money."

"I agree." The normal thing was for the string that actually did the job to repay the financer two hundred percent, if the job worked out. The risk was high enough to make that kind of repayment necessary. The two thousand Hughes had borrowed would be paid back with four thousand off the top of whatever the job brought in.

"I got a local man," Hughes said. He never looked away from the windshield, but his face changed expressions just as though he were looking at the person he was talking to. "A doctor," he said. "Can you feature that? A guy I know told me about him, two three years ago."

"As a matter of fact," Grofield said, "a guy I've used a couple of times is a doctor, too. In New York. If you ever need any financing there, look him up. Doctor Chester Ormont, on East Sixty-seventh Street in Manhattan."

"My man in St. Louis is Doctor Leon Castelli, on Grove Avenue." Hughes looked a question at the windshield. "How come doctors? I can't figure it."

"Unreported income," Grofield said. "I don't think I've ever worked a job that wasn't financed by somebody's unreported income. There's certain classes of people that tend to get paid in cash, without records, so they don't report their entire earnings to the income tax people. Like doctors, they get a lot of patients that pay cash."

Hughes grinned at the windshield. "Everybody's got a hustle," he said.

"There's safety deposit boxes all over this country," Grofield said, "packed with cash that was never reported to Internal Revenue. And these people can spend a few hundred of it, but if they start to spend in the thousands over their reported income level, they might attract the wrong kind of attention. So it's all just sitting there, in cash, in safety deposit boxes."

"Wouldn't you like the master key?" Hughes asked.

"As a matter of fact, yes."

"But why use that money to finance operations like us? I mean, I know why *we* use the money, but how come they give it to us?"

"They hate to see money lie fallow," Grofield said. "Doctors in particular, they're the investing kind, they like to know their money's out there working for them. The money in the safety deposit box is gravy scooped off the top, they get to keep one hundred cents on every dollar of it, but they want more. They want to see it work, they want to see it bring home some friends."

Hughes shook his head. "What good is it? Money's to spend." He grinned at the windshield. "That's why I'm broke all the time. When I've got it, I party."

"I spend it, too," Grofield said, thinking of his theater.

"But not these doctors, huh? Castelli gives me two grand, it comes out of his safety deposit box. I give him back four grand, the whole bundle goes in the safety deposit box?"

"Probably."

"Then what's the point? If he can't take a chance on spending the two, he sure can't take a chance on spending the four. So what the hell's the point?"

"I don't know," Grofield said. "A different kind of mind from ours."

"Yeah. So that's why they're doctors, and we're—" he shrugged, looking at the windshield "—whatever we are."

That was the end of that conversation. They drove for a while in silence, until Hughes asked if Grofield minded the radio. He said he didn't, and they listened to a hill-billy station after that.

Route 3 would have eventually taken them to the bottom of the state and across into Kentucky if they'd stayed with it, but instead they crossed the river at Cape Girardeau. They picked up 61 there, dropped south again, got onto 62, and cut southwest across the ankle of Missouri, entering Arkansas at St. Francis. Their destination was about ten miles beyond that, near Piggott.

5

It was a pyramid-shaped hill, fairly tall, and the whole side facing the road was strewn with junked cars and parts of cars, all silently rusting in the late afternoon sun. Three smallish trees jutted improbably out of the metal at odd points on the hillside, pale green with the fresh leaves of spring, and a narrow dirt road meandered up through the junk as though a bulldozer had gone through just once, shoving everything out of its way. Up at the top stood an old clapboard farmhouse, two stories high, rambling this way and that over the crest of the hill as though it had melted somewhat from its original shape. The siding was the gray of weathered wood that hasn't been painted for at least a quarter century.

Grofield said, "It's beautiful."

Hughes grinned at the windshield and turned off onto the twin-rut dirt road; it ran level for about a hundred feet, before climbing the hill. "I guess Purgy don't mind it," Hughes said.

They'd come two hundred twenty-five miles in just over four hours; it was now late afternoon, and the sunlight reflecting from windows and windshields up and down the hill was tinged with orange, so that it looked as though rust was reflecting light.

The fence was rusty, too, when they came to it, at the base of the hill. Eight foot high, chain link, it stretched away on both sides, hemming the junked cars in, and topped by a triple strand of barbed wire. The gate was the same height, and also topped by barbed wire, and there was a sign on it that said NO TRESPASSING—*Ring Phone For Entry.*

Hughes left the motor running and got out of the car. He went over to the box mounted on the left gatepost, opened the door, and spent a minute talking on the phone. Grofield waited in the car; he rolled his window down and listened to silence. No birds, nothing but the almost-silent purr of the engine.

Hughes came back to the car and slid behind the wheel.

"Best roll your window up," he said.

Grofield looked at him, but didn't ask any questions. He rolled his window up, and at the same time the two halves of the gate opened inward—electric, remote control.

Hughes drove the Javelin through and started up the hill. Grofield twisted around to watch the gates shut again, and when he faced front there was a Doberman pinscher directly in their path, black, with brown markings.

Hughes was driving slowly up the steep incline, and he neither braked nor hit the horn, but just kept moving toward the dog, which at the last moment padded with heavy gracefulness to one side. It met Grofield's eyes through the closed window as the car went by, and it didn't look sweet-tempered at all.

"Nice playmate," Grofield said.

"Purgy don't get robbed," Hughes said.

"I bet he doesn't."

Grofield looked back, to see if the dog was following

them, and now there were two, both Dobermans, both padding along right behind the car. And as he watched, a third came streaking through narrow alleys amid the junk to the right and joined the first two.

Grofield said, "How many's he got?"

"I don't know. More than enough."

"One is enough," Grofield said, and faced front after that.

There was a little open flat area at the top, in front of the house, and standing in it was a short, fat, very wide man with a bull neck and an irritable expression. He was filthy, clothing and skin and hair, wearing stained gray workpants, black work boots and a flannel shirt that had once been several colors but was now mostly a faded grayish pink. There were so many streaks of rust and grease and dirt over his arms and face and clothes that he almost looked like an Indian in war paint.

Grofield said, "That's got to be Purgy."

"You're right."

Purgy gave them an irritable arm wave, meaning to follow him, and tramped on around the corner of the house. Hughes drove slowly after him, and Grofield saw that they were now surrounded by at least five dogs, one of them trotting along in front. He said, "Is Dobermans all he's got?"

Hughes frowned at the windshield. "I don't follow you."

"The dogs. Are they all Dobermans?"

"Is that what they are? They all look alike, so I guess so."

Purgy had led them along the continuation of the dirt road around the side of the house, and now around to the back. Here the hill fell away more slowly, in broad steps.

The first level below the house contained a dozen or more vehicles of a wide variety of kinds, all in apparently good operating order. The level below that had a rickety shed-like ten-car garage, with several cars and parts of cars on the beaten dirt in front of it, and with the chain-link fence running along just behind it. Beyond the fence were trees, a thick woods that stretched on down into the valley.

"I guess that's our truck," Hughes said.

Grofield nodded. "Looks all right."

"The sound is more important," Hughes commented.

The truck was one of the vehicles on the first level, a big tractor-trailer rig with a dark green International Harvester cab and an unpainted aluminum Freuhauf body. There were no markings on the body, but the cab door bore the legend UNIVERSAL FUR STORAGE, *210–16 Pine Street, Phone 378-9825.*

"It's hot," Grofield said. "It's left over from a hijack."

"I already knew that. That's why we're getting a price."

"Original plates?"

"I brought my own."

"We'll have to do something about that door."

"If we take it."

And if they didn't? This was Thursday; they were supposed to move tomorrow night. Grofield said, "You got any others lined up?"

"Not yet. If this one's no good, it costs us a couple weeks."

Out there in front of them, Purgy was still walking, a steady fat man's waddle. A couple of dogs were flanking him now, and maybe half a dozen of them were around the car. Purgy led them halfway across the rear of the ramshackle house to where the dirt road made a sharp turn downward and to the left, down to the next level. They all went on down there, Purgy and the dogs and the Javelin, making a strange parade, and then headed straight for the fur-storage truck.

"He's going to want us to get out of the car," Grofield said.

"The dogs are okay. They do what Purgy tells them."

Purgy had reached the truck, and now he turned around and made a down-pushing motion with one hand to tell them to stop. Hughes left the engine running, and opened the door, and a second later so did Grofield.

It was very strange. They were waist deep in dogs, and it was like moving through a sluggish black sea full of eyes and teeth. The dogs kept circling, kept moving around without ever making a single noise, and always moved out of the way whenever Grofield or Hughes or Purgy walked anywhere. But Grofield kept being aware of them, down there around his wrists, moving, watching, waiting, and after a while the total absence of sound—no barking, no growling, nothing—became the most nerve-wracking part of it, as though tension were being built that would have to end with incredible noises and destruction.

Purgy and Hughes immediately started talking about the truck, and Grofield did his best to pay attention and not think about the dogs. In the usual manner of buyer and seller, Purgy kept pointing out how good the truck was and Hughes kept suggesting flaws it probably had. "Looks as though she was driven pretty hard," Hughes said, holding the driver's door open and leaning his head in beside the seat. "Look at that brake pedal, how she's worn on the one side. Some cowboy drove the hell out of her."

"Why, that truck's only two years old," Purgy said. He had a high-pitched voice, but very hoarse, as though he'd worn his throat out reaching for high notes. "Barely broke in," he said. "Where you going to find a truck this new at the price I'm asking?"

Grofield stood and watched. This wasn't his specialty; he was along to drive the extra vehicle if they bought the truck.

Hughes looked under the hood. "Got pliers on you?"

"You ain't gonna take it *apart*," Purgy said.

"Just want to take a look. We need a tape measure, too."

"You don't want much," Purgy grumbled, and turned to Grofield. "See that bread truck there? Take a look in the back, there's a toolkit, bring it on over."

"Okay."

"Dogs!" Purgy yelled. "Stay!"

They stayed. Grofield walked across the brown dirt to the bread truck and found the toolkit in the back, and none of the dogs followed him. But when he started back he saw half the dogs back there by Purgy standing absolutely still and watching him. Six or seven of them, that was, with an equal number still moving around Hughes. Grofield carried the toolkit over and put it on the ground by the truck, and the watching dogs started to mill with the others again.

Hughes took the pliers and tape, and handed the tape to Grofield. "Size of the opening in back," he said.

"Right."

The inevitable three or four dogs traveled with him as he went around to the back of the truck and opened the doors there. He climbed up into the trailer, and was half-surprised that none of the dogs leaped up after him.

The interior of the trailer was bare, except for two pipes running the length of it just above head level. To hang furs on, probably. Grofield measured the opening, spent a minute walking around the interior, stamping on the floor, pushing against the walls, and then he dropped down amid the dogs again and went back to where Hughes and Purgy were arguing over a sparkplug in Hughes' hand. Purgy was saying, "I give you this truck the way it come to me. I don't switch sparkplugs, I don't set back the mileage, I don't do nothing. It's yours, the way the guy drove it in here, for two grand."

Hughes said, "Now you know I'm not gonna pay two thousand dollars for this truck."

"Where you gonna get a truck like this?"

"As hot as this? Nowhere." He turned and looked questioningly at Grofield.

Grofield said, "Fifty-seven inches wide, eighty-four inches high."

"Narrow," Hughes said. "I'm not sure we can use it at all."

"You don't want to buy the truck," Purgy said, "nobody's got a gun to your head."

Grofield said to Hughes, "The floor seems okay."

Hughes nodded and leaned in at the engine.

Purgy said, "What are ya doin *now?*"

"Putting it back."

With Hughes showing him nothing but back, Purgy turned to Grofield. "You know trucks?"

"They're bigger than cars," Grofield said. "That's about my limit."

"Well, believe me, this truck is a steal at two grand."

"You mean it's stolen," Hughes said, his voice muffled because he was still involved with the engine. He surfaced, turning back to Purgy with his hands out in front of him. "You got a cloth to wipe my hands?"

"Up on the seat of the truck. Go on up, start the engine, listen to it."

"I believe I will," Hughes said, and climbed up into the cab. While Grofield and Purgy watched and waited, Hughes started the engine, switched it off, started it, switched it off, started it, raced it, switched it off, started it, lurched the truck forward about three feet, switched it off, started it, lurched it backward about three feet, switched it off, started it, and drove it away.

Grofield watched it leave. About half the dogs stayed with him and Purgy, and the rest went trotting off with the truck.

Hughes was a first-rate driver. There wasn't that much room to maneuver in among the cars and trucks and buses and odd vehicles stored on this flat area, but Hughes threaded the maze with no trouble at all. He backed in a figure eight, he drove forward in various directions at various speeds and in various gears, and finally he drove it back over to Purgy and Grofield again, jolted to a stop, and switched off the motor.

Purgy had his hands on his hips, ready to be belligerently defensive about the truck. He watched Hughes climb down from the cab and said, "Well?"

"Brakes grab to the right a bit," Hughes said. "Trailer doesn't track very well."

"It's empty, what do you want from it? You know a truck like that isn't meant to drive empty."

"It's worth five hundred, I suppose," Hughes said carelessly.

"Five *hundred!* Are you out of your mind? Don't you want me to even get my cost back?"

"I've sold you things," Hughes said. "I know what your cost is. You maybe paid a hundred and a half for this—"

"Hughes, you're a goddam fool. Who's gonna sell a truck like that for a hundred and fifty dollars?"

"The people that brought it to you," Hughes said. "They made their money out of what was in it. All they wanted is a safe place to unload it, and not leave it off a road someplace for the cops to pick up and maybe find somebody's fingerprints or coat button or something. I told you, I've *sold* you stuff. So you paid a hundred and a half. If you take it apart and sell the pieces you can sell and junk the rest, you'll maybe make three hundred out of it."

"There's another dumb idea," Purgy said, trying to be scornful but only being irritable. "There's better than three hundred just under the hood alone."

"But we're saving you the trouble," Hughes said. "You don't have to do any work on it at all, you don't have to store the parts, you don't do anything but spend five minutes out here having a nice talk with me, and you make better than two hundred percent profit. That isn't bad."

"I told you my price," Purgy said. Now he sounded as though he'd been insulted.

"Oh, you didn't mean a number like that," Hughes said. "That was just to argue from. But it's getting late in the day, we've got a long drive ahead of us, so I figured I'd go straight to the sensible price. Five hundred."

"Now look," Purgy said, "you're an old customer and I

like you, and I know you like this here truck. So I'll give you a break. I paid twelve hundred for that truck, and I'll give it to you for fifteen. Now, that's fair, isn't it?"

"Oh, come on, Purgy. You didn't pay any twelve hundred and we both know it. Now, why say a thing like that?"

"Well, I wouldn't if it wasn't so."

"Then it's the first time I ever saw you get took, and I can't take the truck. Come on, Grofield."

Hughes started toward the Javelin, Grofield beside him.

Purgy shouted, "Hughes, goddam it, are you tryin' to make me mad?"

Grofield suddenly became doubly aware of all those dogs, milling around between there and the Javelin. Did they want to make Purgy mad? Did they want to dicker with a man who had all those dogs around? What if he told the dogs not to let you go until you met his price? Grofield put his hands in his pockets, not wanting his fingers to stray accidentally into any passing dog's mouth.

Purgy shouted, "Hughes, you just stop goddam it where you stand!"

Hughes stopped, and turned around, and looked at Purgy. "You've always been a tough bargainer, Purgy," he said, "but you've never told me an out-and-out lie before. Twelve hundred dollars. Why, man, my three-year-old daughter wouldn't believe that."

Grofield looked at him. Three-year-old daughter?

Purgy suddenly grinned. "Aw, Hughes, you're such a dumb bastard. I've lied to you plenty."

"Not such obvious lies, then," Hughes said. "Listen, so we don't get mad at each other, I'll go eight hundred."

"You'll go eleven hundred and no more arguing,"

Purgy said. "And don't talk to me about a thousand, because eleven hundred is my bottom number."

Hughes said, "For eleven hundred, you can paint the goddam owner's name off the doors."

"Eleven hundred like she stands."

"I *will* walk away from here, Purgy," Hughes said. Grofield looked sideways at him, and Hughes' profile was grim and angry. There was no mistaking it; Hughes was mad, and ready to stomp away no matter how good the truck was.

Purgy didn't say anything for a minute, and Grofield, studying him, saw that Purgy too was on the edge of real anger. Grofield waited, knowing better than to enter into this thing, but hoping one or the other of them would eventually climb down off his ultimatum. It would be really stupid to have to wait around St. Louis an extra fifteen days because of no truck, with a perfectly good truck standing right there.

Finally, Purgy sighed. He shook his head, and shrugged his fat shoulders, and said, "I don't see any damn reason to get upset. What the hell, if I can't bend a little what am I in business for? I'll spray a little paint over those doors for you."

"Dark green," Hughes said.

"Well, it may not be a Grade A Perfect one hundred percent match," Purgy said, "but I'll give it the closest I got."

Hughes suddenly nodded; his face and body became more relaxed. "It's a deal," he said.

"That's fine," Purgy said, with a broad smile. "I'll go get the paint."

"We've got our own plates to put on," Hughes said.

"Well, go ahead."

Purgy waddled away toward the house, and Hughes said, "Come on." He and Grofield went over to get the plates out of the trunk of the Javelin. They were Missouri plates, for a commercial vehicle, and they weren't on anybody's wanted list. "These babies cost me a hundred and a quarter," Hughes said, taking them out. "And now I went a hundred over what I wanted to pay for the truck."

"I thought you were going to walk away," Grofield said. "I really did."

Hughes looked at him in surprise. "You did? What the hell would I do that for? The truck's worth fourteen."

"You looked mad."

"It took you in, huh? I don't think it took Purgy in."

"I do," Grofield said.

"Purgy's slier'n he looks," Hughes said. He gave Grofield one of the plates and a screwdriver. "You do the back, I'll do the front."

"Right."

They walked together toward the truck. Hughes said, "I hope Barnes makes a good price on the guns. We'll go over the two grand if we're not careful."

They separated at the rear of the truck, where Grofield hunkered down to remove the Pennsylvania plate the truck was carrying. A couple of dogs came over to watch, but by now Grofield was getting used to them—silent, restless, observant, more like an audience in a theater than anything else.

He was just finishing removing the Pennsylvania plate when Purgy came back down from the house, shaking a can of spray enamel in one fist. The metal stirring ball rattled around inside it. Grofield put the clean Missouri plate on, picked up the Pennsylvania plate, and walked over to see what the spray job looked like.

It was a slightly lighter shade of green, but Purgy was doing a pretty good job of bleeding it out at the edges. It would be plain that a firm name had been removed, but it would look like a neat job, not something done in a sloppy hurry.

Hughes came over with the other plate and the other screwdriver and studied the door. Purgy, finished, stepped back and said, "How's that? Nice, huh?"

"I won't argue with you, Purgy," Hughes said, as though he thought the paint job was lousy.

But Purgy was in a good mood now, and didn't care what Hughes said. "You just didn't want to pay me so much," he said, grinning. "I know you, Hughes."

"What about the other door?"

"Keep your pants on, I'm gonna do it right now. And then you got to pay me."

"You keep your pants on, too."

Purgy went around to the other side of the truck, and Hughes said to Grofield, reluctantly, "I suppose I'd better drive the truck. Get to know it and all."

"Don't worry," Grofield said. "I'll treat your car like a bride."

"I don't think I'd like that," Hughes said.

"You know what I mean."

"Let me go first," Hughes said. "You just stay at my pace."

"Sure."

Hughes gave him the license plate and screwdriver. "We'll stop somewhere and eat. I know a couple places."

"Fine."

Hughes looked across at his car, and then at Grofield. He wanted to give Grofield an hour or two of instructions about how to handle the car; Grofield waited and watched him fight the urge and win. "See you later," Hughes said.

"See you later," Grofield said. He turned and walked toward the Javelin, his hands full of license plates and screwdrivers. Dogs were loping all around him. He found he was grinning at the car.

6

A match flared in the darkness—Ed Barnes, lighting a cigarette. In the yellow light, Grofield could see the three of them sitting on the floor of the empty truck, himself and Barnes and Steve Tebelman, and the big sheet of plywood leaning against the end wall, two lengths of clothesline stretching across it to keep it in place. "That's really a nice job," he said, looking at what was painted on the plywood.

"Thanks," Tebelman said. Barnes shook the match out, and they were in darkness again. There was a faint redness when Barnes drew on the cigarette, but not enough to show more than vague outlines.

"You're a talented guy," Grofield said. "You ought to be able to make a living out of that."

"Commercial art?" Tebelman's voice dripped with scorn.

"Oh," Grofield said.

Barnes said, "An artist." He said it with no particular intonation, as though simply describing a condition of life.

"I understand that," Grofield said. "I'm into something like that myself."

"You are?"

Grofield heard the interest in Tebelman's voice, and was tempted to go into a whole explanation about being an actor in a pre-technological sense—he had the feeling Tebelman's attitudes would be basically similar—but something about the presence of Barnes, his cigarette a red dot in the darkness, inhibited him. Barnes, he knew, was the more typical heister; a professional with only this one profession, who found all his satisfactions, financial and otherwise, within the one area. Tebelman was the only other person like himself Grofield had ever met in this business.

And Tebelman's question was hanging in the darkness, awaiting an answer. More conscious of Barnes' presence than he would have been in a lighted room where he could see the man, Grofield said, "I'm an actor. I own a summer theater."

"Isn't there money in that?"

"Hardly. Not with movies and television."

"Ah." There was a little silence, then, until Tebelman said, "You know, there's a school of thought that says the artist and the criminal are variants on the same basic personality type. Did you know that?"

Grofield was sorry now the conversation had gotten started at all. "No, I didn't," he said.

"That art and crime are both antisocial acts," Tebelman said. "There's a whole theory about it. The artist and the criminal both divorce themselves from society by their life patterns, they both tend to be loners, they both tend to have brief periods of intense activity and then long periods of rest. There's a lot more."

"Interesting," Grofield said. He wished Hughes would start them moving; he held his left hand up near his face, pushed the sleeve back, read the radium dial of his watch. Ten minutes to eleven. He knew Hughes was waiting for the county sheriff's car to come by. The truck they were sitting in was parked in a closed-for-the-night gas station a quarter mile from the Food King store. Once the sheriff's department car went by, they'd have a minimum of twenty minutes before that car would come around again to the Food King parking lot. So Hughes was waiting for it, and once it was safely out of the way they would start to move.

Tebelman was saying, "Of course, there've been a lot of artists who were criminals first, like Jean Genêt. But you and I reverse that, don't we? You're an actor, and I'm a painter."

"That's right," Grofield said.

Barnes suddenly said, "I'm quite a reader, you know." The heavy voice, calm and uninflected, was a total surprise; it didn't seem to convey any emotion at all, nothing but the information contained in the words, the same as when he had earlier said that Tebelman was an artist.

Grofield stared at the red cigarette end. He had no idea how to take what Barnes had said. Maybe if he could see the man's face...

Tebelman had apparently decided to take it straight. "Is that right?" he said.

"I started in Joliet," Barnes said. "You have a lot of time on your hands in a place like that."

Under cover of darkness, Grofield permitted himself to grin.

Tebelman said, "A lot of artists got started in prison, just for that reason. Like O. Henry."

"I really took to it," Barnes said. "Now I read three, four books a week."

"Is that right?"

"Westerns," Barnes said. "Ernest Haycox, Luke Short. Some of these newer ones, too, Brian Garfield, Elmer

Kelton. Some parts of the country it's tough to find them."

Tebelman said, "Did you read *Sliphammer*?"

"Did I!"

The truck suddenly jerked into motion. "We're off," Grofield said. But Tebelman and Barnes were talking about Westerns.

7

In most supermarkets, the male clerks restock the shelves with merchandise after the close of business on Friday evening in preparation for the volume they expect to do on Saturday. In a large store, this restocking can take as much as six or seven hours, starting at a nine P.M. closing and continuing through most of the night. The Food King outside Belleville, Illinois, was no exception.

Deliveries to supermarkets after closing hour on Friday are unusual but not unheard of, and so the tractor-trailor that drove into the Food King parking lot at two minutes to eleven P.M. on Friday the eleventh of April seemed perfectly ordinary and legitimate. The cab of the truck was green, the body aluminum. There was no firm name on either.

The truck drove around to the rear of the store, and the driver backed it up to the loading platform. He switched off the motor, picked up a clipboard, got out of the cab, and walked down the length of the truck to the loading platform. He wore a zippered jacket, a peaked cap, and a yellow pencil stub behind one ear; these three things, and the clipboard, made his face invisible.

There were wooden steps at the side of the loading platform. The driver went up them and pushed the button next to the corrugated metal garage-type door. He waited two minutes, and was about to ring again when the door began to slide upward. It slid about five feet and stopped. A clerk in a white shirt and a knee-length white apron, a prematurely balding man of about thirty-five, very slender, ducked and came out to the platform. Over the door a pipe came out with a conical metal reflector at the end and a fairly dim light bulb in it; the only source of light other than the truck lights, which the driver had left on.

The clerk said, "What is it?"

"Delivery."

"They didn't tell me about it." He was probably more than a clerk, he was probably the assistant manager. He sounded peeved that he hadn't been told about the delivery.

The driver shrugged and said, "Don't ask me, Mac. I just drive where they tell me to drive." He tapped the clipboard with a knuckle.

"Nobody ever gets anything straight around here. Hold on."

The clerk went back inside, ducking under the partly opened door, and a few seconds later the door rose the rest of the way. Inside was a high-ceilinged room with a cement floor, about the size of a one-car garage. Trash barrels lined the righthand wall. Conveyor-belt sections were stacked on the lefthand wall. There were two doors out of the room, one in the righthand corner of the far wall and one in the lefthand wall, down at the other end. The clerk was standing in the door to the left, calling, "Tommy! Red!" He called the names twice more, then turned and came back to the loading platform. "They'll be right here."

"I got all night," the driver said. He acted bored.

"Anything refrigerated on there?"

"No, not this truck."

Two more clerks came through the lefthand door and hurried out to the loading platform. Both were around twenty years old. The tall, thin one with red hair would probably be Red, which would make the middleweight with hornrim glasses and black hair Tommy.

Tommy said, "What've we got?"

"Nothing refrigerated," the assistant manager-type said. "We'll just unload it straight into the trash room here and leave it till we're done out front. Then we'll put it away in the stockroom." He turned to the driver, who was mostly behind them all, leaning against the side of the doorway. "Do you want to open it for us?"

"It isn't locked."

"I got it," Tommy said, and reached for the rear doors of the truck.

8

"Don't make a move," Grofield said. Hooded, holding the machine gun, he stepped out of the back of the truck on to the loading platform and took a quick step to the left. Beyond the three pale stunned faces, he saw Hughes hurry into the building and on down to stand by the left-hand door, where he put the clipboard down on the floor and pulled his hood and pistol out of his jacket.

It was the older assistant manager-type who recovered first. Slowly lifting his hands, he said, "We won't cause you any trouble. We don't have guns."

"I should think not," Grofield said. "Go on into the truck, you and you." Pointing the gun barrel at the two younger clerks.

They both hung back. The older clerk said, "Do what they tell you to do. You can't fight guns."

Barnes was standing in the truck doorway, holding the other machine gun. "That's sensible," he said, and his heavy voice seemed full of menace. "None of us wants to kill anybody. All we're here for is money. You people cooperate, you'll live happily ever after."

"We'll cooperate," the older clerk said. "Go on, Tommy. Red? Go on."

The younger ones still hesitated, not because they had it in mind to fight back, but because they were afraid. And why not? They were facing three men wearing black hoods over their faces, two carrying machine guns. And

Tebelman, deeper in the truck, was standing there with clothesline in his hands.

Grofield said, "You're just getting a long smoke break, that's all. Nothing to worry about. Go on in."

Red moved first, and a second later Tommy followed. While Barnes watched over them, Tebelman would have them remove their aprons and then he'd tie their hands behind them, sit them down, tie their ankles, and blindfold them. There was no need to gag them; a man who can't see won't shout.

Meantime, Grofield said to the older clerk, "What's your name?"

"Harris." He was frightened, but trying to deal with the situation as though it were matter-of-fact, as though the best way to handle it was to be quiet and calm and methodically obedient. Which was true.

"I mean your first name," Grofield said. He'd learned this a few years ago, from somebody else in the business—when you have people to control during a job, find out their first names and then call them by name every chance you get. You acknowledge their individuality that way, you suggest that you accept their personal worth, and they become less afraid that you're going to hurt or kill them.

The clerk said, "Walter."

"What do they call you? Walt? Wally?"

"Just Walter." He sounded depressed by the fact.

Grofield said, "Okay, Walter. How many more employees are in the store?"

"Four."

"Just seven of you tonight? How come?"

"We always have just seven," Walter said. "We're the regular night crew."

"Okay. What are the first names of the other four?"

"Hal and Pete and Andy and Trig."

"Trig?"

"It's a nickname. He's Anthony Trigometrino."

"Okay. Where are they? All four out by the shelves?"

"No, Trig's in the stockroom. The others are out front."

"And where's the stockroom?"

Walter made a vague gesture in the general direction of Hughes. "Through that door…down there."

"Okay, Walter. You and I are going to walk down there, and you're going to stick your head through the doorway and ask Trig to come out here for a minute. Got that?"

Walter nodded. "I'll do it."

"You won't say anything dumb."

"No, sir," Walter said. His nervousness was increasing again.

Grofield didn't want anybody getting over-emotional. He didn't like to do that to people unnecessarily, in the first place, and in the second place a calm person tended to cause less trouble. He said, "Walter, I'm sorry if I make you nervous. There's nothing I can do about the gun and the mask. But you know all we care about is the cash in the safe, right?"

Walter nodded.

"And you know we'd rather not have the police looking for us for shooting somebody."

"I guess so," Walter said.

"Take my word for it, Walter. We'll make this whole thing as easy as we can for everybody. Now, let's go down to the door there."

"All right," Walter said. He seemed somewhat calmer.

They went down by the door. Hughes was masked now, and carrying a Smith & Wesson Centennial .38 with a grip safety; a bar on the back of the grip had to be depressed before the revolver could be fired.

Hughes stepped two quick paces back from his post beside the doorway and whispered. "There's somebody in the next room. I think it's just one."

"That's Trig," Grofield whispered. "Walter's going to call him out now. Go ahead, Walter. Tell him to come out here for a minute, and then step back and leave the doorway clear. Got it?"

"Yes," Walter said. He was matter-of-fact, and he'd dropped the "sir," which was good. It meant he wasn't afraid of being killed any more.

Grofield and Hughes stood beside the wall, Grofield in front because the machine gun was more persuasive to look at than a small revolver, and Walter went over and stood in the doorway. He called, "Trig?" A voice called something back, and Walter said, "Come on out here a minute, will you?"

Grofield could make out what the voice said this time: "*Now* what? I got all this stuff piled up here—"

Trig came through the doorway still grousing, and was a full two strides into the room before he noticed Grofield and Hughes and the guns. He'd started griping at Walter, saying, "How do you expect me to get my—" Then he stopped dead, mouth and feet, and stared at the gun.

Grofield said, "Keep walking, Trig. Don't do anything excitable."

Trig was heavyset, medium height, and very hairy. He looked to be in his late twenties, and wore black slacks and a white T-shirt. No apron. His arms were thick and hairy, and he had initials tattooed on the left upper arm: AT–VC. He had a heavy sullen face, with thick blue beard shadow. He was the kind who does excitable things and louses everybody up and gets himself killed.

The idea was to keep things moving. Grofield said, "Walter, walk on over to the corner over there, by the other door. Trig, walk on out to the truck. Go on out by Red and Tommy."

The idea behind moving Walter away was to leave Trig the only one not standing next to a wall. Completely alone in the middle of the concrete floor, Trig looked this way and that, his shoulder muscles bunching but his brain unable to decide where or how he should jump. And as he continued to look around, to see Hughes behind Grofield, to see Barnes with another machine gun at the entrance to the truck, to see Tommy and Red already trussed up and sitting on the truck floor, Trig's tensed shoulders slowly lowered, his half-clenched fists relaxed, and all he did after all was say, "You jerks won't get away with this."

"Then it would be even sillier for you to get killed over it," Grofield said. "Walk on out to the truck, Trig."

Trig went. He walked slowly, to show he wasn't being pushed around.

Grofield turned his attention back to Walter. "The three outside," he said. "Hal and Pete and Andy. Will they be coming to the stockroom?"

"To get more goods to bring out front, yes."

"Fine. Come along with me, Walter."

Hughes stayed back in the first room, by the door. Grofield and Walter went into the stockroom, a long high-ceilinged area piled high with boxes and cartons, some of the stacks reaching up eight or nine feet and forming aisles in between.

There were double swinging doors leading out to the store, with a small window at eye level in each. Grofield peered through one of these, saw the store brightly lit but none of the clerks visible, and turned back to look at the storeroom and set the scene.

"Walter," he said, after a minute, "you sit over there on those bags of dog food. Go ahead."

Walter went over, puzzled but obedient, and sat down. He was now about eight feet from the swinging doors, and clearly visible to anyone who'd come through there. He was a bit to the left of the doors, toward the other room, where Hughes was waiting.

Grofield nodded, satisfied, and went to stand against the wall to the right of the doors. "Now, Walter," he said, "as each of them comes in, I want you to say his name, and then say, 'There's a problem. We have to do what these people say.' Got it?"

Walter repeated what Grofield had said.

"Good," Grofield said. "But with the name in front of it. If it was Andy, for instance—you'd say, 'Andy, there's a problem. We have to do what these people say.' See what I mean?"

" 'Andy, there's a problem. We have to do what these people say.' "

It was just like blocking out a scene on stage, really, and using local amateur talent. No different, and no more difficult. "That's fine, Walter," Grofield said. Always praise your local amateur talent. "Now let's relax. You can smoke if you want."

"I don't smoke. I gave it up."

"Smart. I did, too. Why shorten our lives, right, Walter?"

Walter gave a pale smile.

They had to wait three minutes before any of the clerks came back, pushing their stock carts through the swinging doors, but then it went like clockwork. The one called Pete came through first. Walter gave him the line, Pete took in the hood and the machine gun, and Grofield sent him over to the farther door, where Hughes picked him up—like a bucket brigade, it was—and sent him on to the truck. There, Barnes kept an eye on him while Tebelman lashed him and stashed him with the rest.

Andy came through a minute after Pete, and followed the same assembly line. But then five minutes went by, and finally Grofield said, "Walter, I'm afraid you're going to have to call Hal in here. Just get up and push one of those doors open and call him to come in. Then go back and sit down, and we'll do it just like we did with the other two."

Walter obeyed, and a minute later Hal joined the bucket brigade.

"And now you, Walter," Grofield said. "I want to thank you for your cooperation."

"I didn't want any of the boys working for me to get hurt," Walter said. He was apparently trying out the line he would use tomorrow when he explained to his bosses why he didn't get himself killed keeping the store from being robbed.

"That was best," Grofield said. "Go on over there now."

Walter went through the assembly line, Grofield and then Hughes following him. Grofield left the machine gun leaning against the wall just inside the building, and while Barnes watched Tebelman tie and blindfold Walter, Grofield and Hughes took the ropes off that were holding the plywood against the end of the truck. They picked the plywood up and carried it down the length of the truck and out through the rear entrance, having to tilt it at a diagonal to get it through.

The door into the stockroom was an even tighter squeeze. They couldn't get it through at all at first. Grofield said, "This is the one part we didn't case ahead of time."

"How could we?" Hughes asked. He sounded irritable. "Hold on a second. Hold the plywood."

One edge rested on the floor. Grofield held the plywood vertical while Hughes took a screwdriver from his hip pocket and took the door off. That gave them the extra inch they needed, and they slid the plywood through, listening to it scrape at top and bottom.

Barnes and Tebelman joined them. They had closed the rear doors of the truck and shut the overhead door leading to the loading platform. Tebelman was carrying Grofield's machine gun and four aprons.

In the stockroom, they took off their hoods and jackets and donned the aprons. They were all wearing white shirts, and now they were supermarket clerks. Grofield this evening had sideburns and a bushy mustache, and had done a light makeup job on his nose and on the flesh under his eyes. He didn't want to be on stage some night, in his other profession, and have a member of the audience suddenly jump up and shout, "You were one of the robbers at the Food King Supermarket in Belleville, Illinois!" Aside from anything else, it would beat hell out of his timing. And characterization.

There was much less trouble getting the plywood

through the double swinging doors. Grofield, walking backwards, said, "You got the hammer?"

Hughes, carrying the other end, said, "Steve has," and Tebelman said, "I've got it right here."

A large sheet of poster paper covered the face of the plywood, and it made small flapping noises now as Grofield and Hughes carried it down the side aisle toward the front of the store. Tebelman and Barnes had gone the other way, to the produce section, where they knew the store kept its ladder.

With a small and unobtrusive camera, Steve Tebelman had taken several pictures in this store in the last few days, a few of them of the advertising poster atop the safe, the one touting the store's own brand of canned fruits and vegetables. That poster had been recreated with perfect attention to detail on the paper stretched over the face of the piece of plywood.

Grofield and Hughes carried the plywood down to the front of the store, between the first cash register and the manager's office, through the little gate in the wrought iron fence keeping customers away from the safe, and at last leaned it against the wall of the manager's office facing the windows and the parking lot outside. There were three cars in the lot, belonging to the clerks working here tonight. Hughes, looking out the window past the signs advertising specials, said, "No change. Same as when I drove in."

Grofield looked at his watch. "We've got about five minutes before that sheriff's car is due again."

"Plenty of time," Hughes said, and Barnes and Tebelman showed up with the ladder. "Steve, give me the hammer."

"Right here."

Hughes took the hammer. Out of his shirt pocket he brought two wide-headed nails, and gave one to Grofield. Meantime, Barnes and Tebelman set up the ladder next to the window in front of the safe. Tebelman went away to the right and took one of the signs down from one of the other windows and brought it back with him. Barnes went up three steps on the ladder, and started to fuss with the signs. Tebelman put his back against the window and stood there between window and ladder, holding the sign outstretched between his hands. Tebelman, Barnes, the ladder, and the sign Tebelman was holding, all combined with the two signs already pasted to the window, made it impossible for anyone outside to see the safe.

Grofield and Hughes picked up the piece of plywood and moved it over in front of the safe. Two metal bars had been fastened to the back of the plywood, at about waist height, one extending two inches out the left side, the other extending two inches out the right. There was a hole in each. While Grofield held the plywood in place, Hughes hammered a nail through the hole in the bar on the left and into the partition where it began at the edge of the safe. Then he handed the hammer to Grofield, who drove the other nail in on the other side.

Tebelman said, "Hurry up, my arms are getting tired."

Barnes, who was looking out the window between the signs, said, "There's nobody out there at all."

Grofield picked a corner of the poster paper with a fingernail, and then ripped a length of paper off the plywood. Hughes ripped some more off, and the two of them stripped all the paper away. Underneath, Tebelman had painted a lifelike imitation of the front of the safe.

Standing directly in front of it, one could see it was a painting, but somebody in a car out in the parking lot wouldn't give it a second thought.

"Done," Hughes said.

"Fine," Tebelman said, and went away to put the sign back in the window he'd taken it from.

Barnes said, "I'll get my tools. You boys go to work." He folded up the ladder and took it away.

Hughes and Grofield went back around the manager's office to the corner where the potato chips were displayed. They took the racks off the wall and put them out of the way and then, with hammer and screwdriver, began to remove the partition separating them from the back of the safe.

They had it half stripped away by the time Barnes and Tebelman came back, Barnes carrying a crowbar in one hand and a toolkit in the other.

Tebelman said, "Pity you can't just go in through the back."

"The door's best," Barnes said. "Even with the pulling we got to do, it'll wind up a lot faster. You don't know how they build the sides of these boxes."

"I'll take your word for it," Tebelman said.

Grofield said, "Could I borrow your bar for a minute?"

"Sure."

Barnes handed it over, and Grofield hit a two-by-four horizontal support three times. The third time, it popped loose at the left end. "There."

Hughes grabbed the loose end of the two-by-four, pulled it outward away from the safe, and the final third of the partition sprang free. He and Tebelman dragged it down the side aisle out of the way. They were being careful not to leave any of their debris where it could be seen from out front.

Grofield had to use the crowbar again—a two-by-four was nailed to the floor within the partition. Grofield pried it up a bit at a time, and finally Barnes and Hughes together pulled it upward until it snapped at a point to the right of the section they were clearing.

And there was the back of the safe, black metal, hulking, looking as though it weighed a ton and would be neither breached nor moved.

Tebelman said, "That sheriff's car is gonna come around. We'd better show people stocking shelves."

"You people get to it," Barnes said. "I'll get this baby ready to move."

9

22 22 22 22 22 22 22.

Grofield thought, *I must be crazy. What the hell am I stamping the prices on these things for?*

But he couldn't help it. He couldn't knowingly do a bad job; stamp the wrong price on each can, put the canned goods on the wrong shelves, put them up with no prices stamped on them at all. He had found the spot where Hal had been working, and had simply continued where Hal had left off. Spaghetti sauce. Twenty-two cents. Therefore: 22 22 22 22 22 22 22.

Light flickered at the perimeter of his vision. He turned his head and saw headlights sweeping across the parking lot out in front of the store. He was in the middle of the middle aisle, standing there next to the stock cart, the price stamper in his hand, the purple inkpad open in the stock cart's tray. The shelves on both sides of him—*what did they call them? gondolas?*—they were higher than his head, but the aisle itself was rather wide and had a pale cream vinyl tile floor. He felt both exposed and hemmed in, that he could be seen but he couldn't see, and it was difficult not to turn his back on those headlights and the expanse of windows.

I am a stock clerk, he thought. *I must stay in character.* For a long while, he had tended to visualize dramatic situations around himself wherever he might be, as though he were in a movie—even though he would never actually consent to appear in a movie—complete with sound effects and soundtrack music and cliché storylines. He'd drifted out of that habit in the last couple of years, maybe since getting his own theater, but now he consciously did it again, bringing back the old habit for the sake of calming his nerves and helping himself stay in character.

A spy movie. The Russians are watching the embassy, of course, and are confident they'll track down the daring American spy before he manages to turn over the information. What they don't know is that the spy has had a liaison of a romantic nature—ski lodge, fireplace, snow heavy on the roof, a wolf howling in the distance—with the embassy cook, a charming girl who is now his willing slave. And every day she comes to this market for fresh flounder. Today, with the flounder, she will receive—the microfilm!

But the headlights are approaching across the deserted parking lot. Has the NKVD learned what he's up to? The American spy, secure in his disguise as a simple stock clerk, goes on pricing the cans of spaghetti sauce.

22 22 22 22 22 22 22.

10

Two feet up from the floor, the back of the safe had sprouted a hook. It was a large thick hook, on a round metal base pressed flat against the metal surface of the safe. Barnes was in the process of looping two fifteen-foot lengths of chain over the hook. There were padded handholds at each end of each chain.

Grofield said, "You're sure that glue's gonna stick? I'd feel like a damn fool if we all of us started pulling and the hook popped off and we all fell on our butts."

Barnes said, "You ever see the demonstration where they glue a hook to the roof of a car, and then a crane picks up the car by the hook? Well, it's this glue. It's an industrial glue, pressure sensitive type, and there is no way on earth you could take that hook off that safe. You could get cars pulling in opposite directions, and the back of the safe would buckle outward before that hook would come off."

"You know your business," Grofield said.

"That's just what I do."

Each of them took an end of chain, and they spread out backwards until the chains were taut. Barnes said, "We give pressure together, when I say heave."

Everybody got set, leaning backward, feet apart, both hands wrapped around the padded grip.

"Heave!"

It didn't move. Grofield pulled, feeling the muscles

stretch in his shoulders, and nothing happened. They all relaxed again, looking at one another.

"Heave!"

Tebelman shouted, "It moved that time! I felt it!"

"About a quarter inch," Barnes said. He sounded disgusted. "Come on, let's get that goddam thing out of there. Heave!"

Two inches.

"Heave!"

Each time, as more of the safe was on the smooth vinyl flooring and less remained on the rougher concrete flooring it had been standing on, it got a little easier, and they managed to pull it a little farther. When it was about halfway out they stopped for a three minute rest—working their shoulders and arms, walking around a little—and Grofield felt as stiff as though he'd been in a football game. Then they went back to it, and pulled the safe out the rest of the way, and for some reason when they were done pulling Grofield felt physically better than before, not worse.

The others seemed affected the same way. Maybe it was the sudden knowledge that the idea of the heist was going to work out. The painted safe-front was still in place, ready to fool anyone who would look in the window. The safe itself was back where it could be gotten at, out of sight of any window.

They had pulled it a good foot and a half away from the line of the partition, so Barnes would have enough room to work in. Now he picked up his toolkit, a long heavy metal box in dark green, and stepped through the space to stand in front of the safe and study it for a while.

"Fred," he said, "you stick around to help out. You other two guys better go show yourselves; that sheriff's car is gonna come through again pretty soon."

"Right," Grofield said, and he and Tebelman headed away from the safe.

Tebelman said, "We might as well stick together. Two guys working the same aisle will look as natural as anything else."

"Sure," Grofield said. "Come on along."

Behind them, the first squeal of tortured metal sounded.

11

Hughes appeared at the end of the aisle and waved to them. "It's open. Come on."

"Think about it," Grofield said to Tebelman. "We could use a good set designer. Give you something to do summers."

"It might be nice at that," Tebelman said. He and Grofield moved away from the stock cart and walked down the aisle toward Hughes.

It was now close to one o'clock; the sheriff's car had gone by twice since Barnes had started on the safe. Both times, Grofield and Tebelman had been hard at work stocking shelves, moving to a different aisle after each passage of the patrol car, so they'd give the right impression.

Hughes didn't wait for them. He went over to one of the check-out counters, reached underneath, and came up with a couple of shopping bags, the kind with handles. "Looks like a good haul," he said, as Grofield and Tebelman came to the end of the aisle.

Tebelman said, "Good. I could use the money."

"Everybody could use the money," Hughes said.

Barnes was on his knees beside the safe, repacking his toolkit. He had stripped to the waist, and sweat gleamed on his meaty shoulders and chest. He was puffing a little bit, and when the other three arrived he looked up and said, "They really build those mothers."

Grofield took a look. Barnes was an accomplished stripper, and an accomplished stripper leaves a mess behind. The safe door opened from left to right, with the combination at waist height to the left and with the hinges inside on the right. Barnes had found a purchase on the lip of the door at the top left and had gradually forced the metal out and back, like peeling a sardine can. He had stripped open a triangular section of the door, most of the way across the top and down the side almost to the combination. There were three layers of door, each about half an inch thick, and he'd stripped the layers separately. When he'd finished opening the triangular hole, he'd reached in with hammer and chisel and chipped away the combination lock piece by piece, until the numbered face had fallen out onto the floor and the door had sagged quietly open.

Inside were shelves and trays, all metal. The trays contained mostly papers and some rolled coins. The wrapped bundles of money were on the shelves.

Hughes gave the shopping bags to Grofield and Tebelman and stepped in front of the safe. He handed out stacks of bills, and Grofield and Tebelman tucked them away in the shopping bags.

"Roughly sixty grand," Hughes said, at the end.

"That's good enough for me," Barnes said. "Carry my bar, will you, Hughes? Did I leave anything?"

They made sure nothing had been left behind. Barnes carried his toolkit; Hughes, the crowbar; and Grofield and Tebelman, the two shopping bags full of bills.

They left everything temporarily in the stock room while they unloaded Walter and the other clerks from the back of the truck. Working in pairs, they picked each of the clerks up and carried him out of the truck and into the first room in the building, leaving the seven of them sitting in a row along the rear wall. Then they carried the money and tools and guns into the back of the truck and Hughes closed them in and drove them away from there.

There was no talking this time. Grofield spent the time thinking about what he would do with fifteen thousand dollars. A summer of stock could eat ten thousand with no trouble, but the other five was for a vacation. He'd take Mary somewhere, maybe for three weeks. Not now, it was too close to the beginning of the season. In September or October, when the season was over. This time, he would definitely set five thousand aside for a vacation. By September they would both need one.

The truck traveled for twenty minutes, and then stopped. That was about the right length of time, there was nothing to be alarmed about, but Grofield nevertheless reached for the machine gun on the floor beside him in the darkness. He could hear the other two also reaching for guns.

But it was Hughes who opened the doors, and they were where they were supposed to be. Hughes, sounding happier than Grofield had heard him before, called, "How you doing in there?"

"Spent it already," Tebelman said. He sounded happy, too.

Past Hughes, Grofield could see the river, and the shapes of the two cars, Hughes' Javelin and Barnes' Pontiac. Tebelman would leave with Hughes, and Barnes would give Grofield a lift back to the hotel.

They were in the parking lot behind the remains of a burned-out diner just outside Granite City, north of Belleville but still on the Illinois side of the Mississippi. They would leave the truck there. The guns they would throw in the river. The money they would split up now.

Hughes said, "Just wait a minute for me. I'll get our satchels."

"We've got to wait for you," Grofield said. "You've got the light."

Hughes went away and stopped briefly at each of the cars, then came back with his arms full of various kinds of things to carry the money in. Grofield's was the black attaché case.

Grofield stood at the back of the truck and Hughes handed the bags up to him and then climbed up and pulled the doors shut after himself. There were a few seconds of darkness, and then Hughes had his flashlight out of his pocket and switched it on. "Let's get to it."

They all crowded close, and Tebelman counted the money by the light of the pencil flash. It came out to fifty-seven thousand three hundred dollars. They put four thousand to one side; that Hughes would take to repay the doctor who'd financed them. Fifty-three thousand three hundred left. Thirteen thousand three hundred twenty-five dollars each.

"That isn't bad," Grofield said. Nobody disagreed.

12

"Mr. Martin!"

Grofield, on his way by the front desk, stopped and looked at the clerk, feeling suddenly very wary. Barnes' car radio hadn't reported the robbery as yet, but it was ten minutes to three and the alarm should be going out pretty soon. And thirteen thousand dollars was in the attaché case dangling from his right hand.

He moved toward the desk, walking as though his shoes were glass. "Yes?"

"There have been several calls from your wife."

Grofield frowned. "My wife?" Mary knew where he was, naturally, and what name he was using, but she didn't know what the job was or when it would take place.

The clerk had some small papers in his hands. "She called first this morning at nine o'clock, and several times during the day. She wishes you to phone her at once, and she says it is urgent."

There was some sort of undertone in the clerk's voice, something beyond what the words were saying. Grofield, his mind involved in the robbery, took longer than he should have to realize what it meant. "Yes, thank you," he said. "I'll call her." And then he noticed the little smile on the clerk's face, and finally got it; the clerk thought the felony that had been taking place today and tonight was adultery, not larceny. Grofield almost grinned back, but controlled himself. Let the clerk think what he wanted;

any explanation of Grofield's eighteen hour absence other than the true one was fine.

He started away again, and then looked back to say, "I'll probably be checking out in the morning."

The clerk's smile—smirk—widened. "Yes, sir," he said.

Grofield took the elevator up, hurried down the hall to his room—*had something happened to Dan? because of Dan?*—and when he walked in Myers waved a gun at him and smilingly said, "Hello, there, Alan. Nice to see you again."

Grofield shut the door. Myers was smiling, pleased with himself, but the guy with him looked mean-tempered and stupid. He had a gun in his hand, too, but he hardly needed one. He was huge, with the body of a heavy-weight and the head of a cabbage. He said, "About time the bastard got here."

"I'm sure Alan's been busy," Myers said pleasantly. "Planning, planning. A caper is not that easy a thing, Harry. By the way, Harry Brock, Alan Grofield; Alan, Harry. Sit down, Alan."

Grofield put the briefcase on the floor at the foot of the bed and sat down on the bed. Myers was in the room's only chair, and Harry Brock was standing, leaning against the wall beside the window.

Grofield said, "What now, Myers?"

"A visit, Alan. Why be ungracious? In the first place, I owe you thanks. You talked sense to that idiot Leach. If it hadn't been for you, he might still have been carting me around, like the ancient mariner with his albatross. So I thank you."

"You're welcome," Grofield said, sourly. He was thinking

he'd made a mistake with Dan, he should have kept his mouth shut.

"Besides which," Myers said, "I must admit I know you're involved with a caper somewhere around here. And you could use a couple of good men, couldn't you?"

Grofield thought, *I wouldn't use you to collect tickets.* What he said was, "What about that job in Los Angeles? The three old cons and their tunnel?"

Myers grinned in surprise. "Did you go for that one, too? I must be a better liar than I thought."

Harry Brock said, "What three old cons? What tunnel?"

Grofield said, "Myers' last partner, the one whose throat he slit, told him about a—"

Smoothly, Myers said, "That will be enough of that, Alan. There's no point telling Harry silly stories to try to drive a wedge between us. We're partners, and we know we're useful to each other. And we also know we could be useful to you. Tell us about this caper of yours. When's it going to be?"

"It isn't," Grofield said. "It's a washout."

"Oh, nonsense. You've stayed here a week already. You wouldn't do that unless you were planning a job. Where's the job to be?"

The one advantage Grofield had was that Myers knew most jobs were planned far from where they would take place. Myers would be unlikely to guess that this job was right here in the St. Louis area, and was already done.

Tell him a lie? Certainly. Tell him a hundred lies. But not too easily, no point making him suspicious.

Grofield said, "I can't tell you things like that. I have partners, they wouldn't like it."

"Well, now you have two more partners."

"I could bring you around tomorrow," Grofield said. "You could talk to them yourself. But I shouldn't tell you anything tonight."

"Now why would they let us in," Myers said, "unless we already knew the whole thing? Why split with us unless the alternative was to scrub the job? Come on, Alan, you're going to tell us about it before any of us leave this room, so why not do it now?"

Brock said, "Maybe the plans are in that case he brought in with him?"

"No," Myers said. "His part, perhaps, but not the whole thing. Alan isn't an organizer. Who *is* organizing, Alan?"

On that one he could be told the truth. "Fred Hughes."

"Hughes. I don't think I know him. Harry?"

"Never heard of him."

"He drives, too."

"Organizer and driver? Unusual."

Grofield said, "He says we'll probably buy the truck we'll need from a fellow named Purgy."

Myers smiled with recognition. "Up in Arkansas? So where does that put the job? Memphis? Nashville?"

Harry suddenly lifted his arms and brought his hands together. Squeezing his right fist with his left, he made all the knuckles crack. At the same time, he said, "We're doing all the talking. This bird don't talk at all."

"He'll talk. Alan is intelligent, he knows it's best to avoid violence. Don't you, Alan?"

Grofield was thinking, *He got to me through Mary, but she's been calling so he must have left her alive. There may be all kinds of mess up there at the theater, but he did leave her alive.*

"Alan?"

Grofield said, "What?"

"It's time for you to join the conversation," Myers said, and his smile was suddenly wearing thin.

Grofield glanced at Harry, who wasn't smiling at all. It was time to allow himself to be cowed a little. "I can tell you it's in Little Rock," he said.

"Little Rock. And what are you going to do in Little Rock?"

"You know," Grofield said, "you two can give me a bad time tonight if I don't talk, but what if I *do* talk? Then the other guys give me a bad time tomorrow."

"Well, tonight is here," Myers said. "And tomorrow's a long way off. Maybe you ought to just worry about one thing at a time."

Grofield looked over at Harry again, and shook his head. "I don't like this," he said.

"Then get it over with fast," Myers suggested. "Like taking off adhesive tape. One yank and it's done with. What's the thing you're going to do in Little Rock?"

"A bank," Grofield said, reluctantly.

"A bank. Which bank?"

"First National," Grofield said. He didn't know if Little Rock had a First National Bank or not, but most places did, and with any luck Myers wouldn't know Little Rock well enough to be able to catch him in a lie.

"First National," Myers echoed. "Come on, Alan, why do I have to keep asking questions?"

"Well, we don't have the whole operation worked out

yet," Grofield said. He was thinking about the guns he'd helped throw in the Mississippi just an hour ago. He never carried a gun or any other weapon except during a job, and this was one of the very few times in his life he was regretting that. A pistol would be a very nice thing to have right now.

Myers was saying, "I'm not asking about the operation, I'm asking about the bank. Is it the main office? A branch?"

"A branch."

"Where?"

"I don't know, in a suburb someplace. In a shopping center."

"What's the shopping center called?"

"I don't know."

"Well, what's the suburb called?"

Grofield had no idea of the names of Little Rock suburbs. He had to say again, "I don't know."

"He's crapping on us," Harry said. His voice rumbled in his chest. He sounded very irritated.

"It is taking you a long time, Alan," Myers said. "Now, tell me which Little Rock suburb."

"I don't know. I never paid attention, it didn't matter to me."

"We'll let that pass for a minute. But we'll come back to it, Alan. What's your job in it?"

"Crowd control," Grofield said. "That's what I'm good at. I talk to the customers, keep them cooled out, watch them while the others clean out the cages."

"This is a daytime job?"

"Yes."

"In a—"

A sudden siren erupted outside somewhere, interrupting him. Myers looked surprised, and then as the siren receded he grinned and said, "Maybe somebody's working in *this* town tonight." He grew serious again. "In a shopping center, you're pulling a daylight robbery?"

"That's right," Grofield said. He was sweating lightly, he could feel it. Improvisation had never been his strong suit, he'd always preferred to work from a prepared script. The caper he was making up wasn't emerging very well, it didn't have quite the smooth sound of truth.

"So the gimmick," Myers said, "must be in the getaway. What's the brilliant getaway, Grofield?"

Grofield licked his lips, trying to think about brilliant getaways from daylight robberies in shopping centers. "We're starting a fire," he said. "In a…in a hosiery store just down from the bank."

"You're pulling the job dressed as firemen? That's *my* gimmick!" Another siren sounded outside, farther away; Myers turned his head to listen to it, his expression growing thoughtful. Grofield watched Myers' face, sensing what was going on in the brain behind there, and knowing what it meant when Myers' eyes moved and he looked at the attaché case on the floor at the foot of the bed.

Grofield threw an ashtray at Brock and a pillow at Myers, jumped to his feet, grabbed the attaché case, and ran for the door. It took him too long one-handed to get the door open, and both of them were swarming all over him. He kicked and punched, lunging himself backward through the doorway, knowing it was more than the money involved now; Myers would kill him for trying the Little Rock con, there was no question about that.

Myers had both arms wrapped around the attaché case, and Harry Brock was trying to get both arms wrapped around Grofield. Finally there was no longer any choice; Grofield let go the handle of the attaché case. Myers jerked backward into Brock; Grofield tore his arm loose from Brock's fist; and while the two of them in the room sorted themselves out, Grofield ran like hell down the hotel corridor.

Moving

I

Grofield walked into the theater at four in the afternoon, and stood for a second just inside the door, looking down past the rows of seats at the stage. A white sheet was draped over the sofa. Grofield had called here last night, after getting away from Myers and Brock; the conversation had been short, neither of them wanting to say much over the phone, but Grofield had understood from things she said and didn't say that Dan Leach was dead. She had lived here for thirty-four hours now with that thing under the sheet.

Grofield hurried down the aisle and went up the steps to the stage. Mary was on none of the sets, nor in either of the wings. Grofield didn't want to call her name; he didn't know why, exactly, but he just didn't want to shout in here right now. He thought it would be bad for Mary. He found her in the female dressing room, a long narrow room under the stage with one stone wall. She was sitting at the make-up table, doing nothing, and when he walked into the room their eyes met in the mirror and he saw no expression in her face at all. He'd never seen her face so completely empty before, and he thought, *That's what she'll look like in her coffin.* And he ran across the room to pull her to her feet and clamp his arms tightly around her, as though she were in danger of freezing to death and he had to keep her warm.

At first she was unmoving and unalive, and then she

began violently to tremble, and finally she began to cry, and then she was all right.

They were together fifteen minutes before they started to talk. Grofield had made soothing noises and said words to reassure her before that, but there had been no real talk. Now she said, "I don't want to tell you about it. Is it all right?"

"It's all right." She was sitting again, and he was on one knee in front of her, rubbing his hands up and down her arms, still as though trying to keep her warm and alive.

"I don't want to talk about it ever."

"You don't have to. I know what happened; I don't need the details."

She looked at him, and her expression was odd—intense, and somehow sardonic. She said, "You know what happened?"

He didn't understand. They'd come here, Myers and Brock. They'd killed Dan Leach. They'd forced Mary to tell them where Grofield was and what name he was using. What else?

She saw his face change when he realized what else, and she closed her eyes. Her whole face closed, it seemed; it went back to the expression he'd seen when he'd first walked in here.

He pulled her close again. "All right," he said. "All right."

2

Grofield dropped the body in the hole and picked up the shovel again and started pushing the dirt back in. It was a cool night and cloudy, very dark. Despite the chill, Grofield was sweating as he worked. His eyes glared at everything as he moved, his jaw was clenched, his mind was turning and turning and finding no rest.

He finished filling in the grave, returned the pieces of weedy sod to the top, and walked back and forth to tamp the fresh dirt down. Then he walked over to his car, a five-year-old Chevy Nova he'd bought secondhand two years ago, put the shovel and flashlight and ground cloth in the trunk, and drove on back to the theater.

Mary was moving around in bathrobe and slippers, making a midnight snack. They'd made love earlier, downstairs in the dressing room, more awkward with one another than they'd ever been before. The sex had been cumbersome and difficult and not very satisfying in the usual sense, but afterward Mary had been more relaxed, more her normal self. And now that Dan was gone she was even better.

The sofa looked strange. He'd taken the slipcovers off and burned them, but the upholstery itself was stained with blood—Myers had been using his knife again—so Grofield had covered the thing with an old blue bedspread from the storage room downstairs. Under normal circumstances, they would have had their midnight snack sitting on that sofa, but tonight Mary without comment put the things on the table in the dining room set, and Grofield said nothing about it.

She'd made sandwiches and coffee, and she'd put out cookies. They sat at right angles at the table, eating, and Mary started a conversation about the coming season. There were three or four actors from last year they should get in touch with again, people they particularly wanted back. Grofield kept up his part of the conversation and did his best to keep his voice normal and not to glare all the time at the opposite wall. He thought he'd been doing pretty well, when Mary suddenly said, in a matter-of-fact way, "I don't suppose there's any point to my asking you not to go after him."

Grofield looked at her in surprise. "I don't know what to do," he said. "I don't want to leave you here alone."

"I'll go to New York," she said. "Remember, June said we could always stay with her if we came to the city. I'll go there and talk to some of the people we want this year."

"We still don't have the money," Grofield said.

"You'll get it." She said it offhand, as though there were no question.

"You don't mind going to New York?"

"Of course not...Alan?"

He couldn't read her face. "What?"

"Please don't leave tonight," she said. "Please don't leave till tomorrow."

Surprised, he suddenly realized he'd been turning over in his mind various ways to tell her he had to leave right away. As though there were any hurry now. "There's no hurry," he said. Abruptly his face changed; he stopped glaring, and uncovered a natural smile. Reaching out to hold her hand, he said, "I won't leave till you're ready."

3

Grofield put his left foot into the stirrup and stepped up into the saddle. Holding the reins loosely in his left hand, he looked down at the stableman who'd brought this roan mare out to him, and said, "You'll tell Mr. Recklow when he comes back from lunch."

The stableman, a rangy gray-bearded old man who thought he was Gabby Hayes, nodded with a show of exasperation. "I said I would."

"What will you tell him?"

"You're here. Your name is Grofield. You're a friend of Arnie Barrow's."

"That's right." Grofield looked out at the wooded hills extending away beyond the barns. "Where should I wait for him?"

"See that lightning-struck elm down there, end of the meadow?"

"I think so."

"Keep to the left of it, and head up-country. You'll find a waterfall up there."

"Fine," Grofield said. He lifted the reins.

The stableman nodded at the mare's head. "Her name's Gwendolyn."

"Gwendolyn," Grofield said.

"You treat her right," the stableman said, "she'll treat you right."

"I'll remember that." Grofield lifted the reins again, heeled the mare lightly, and she stepped daintily around the sign in front of the barn that read RECKLOW'S RIDING ACADEMY—*Riding Lessons–Hourly Rentals–Horses Stabled.* "Giddyup, Gwendolyn," Grofield said softly. He had never said giddyup to a horse before, but he liked the alliteration.

Gwendolyn turned out to be more spirited than her name, and carried Grofield across the meadow at a fast trot, moving with the eagerness of a puppy let off a leash. Grofield enjoyed her so much he didn't head directly for the waterfall but took her off at an easy lope down a wooded valley spaced with open, sunny fields lush with spring grass. Twice he saw, at a distance, other riders; both times they were moving their mounts at a much more cautious pace than he. East of the Mississippi, horsemanship was becoming a lost art—like cave painting. No wonder Recklow had to supplement the riding academy's income.

When they came to the stream, shallow and rapid over a bed of stones, Gwendolyn expressed a desire to drink. Grofield dismounted and had some of the water himself; it was so cold it made his teeth ache. He grimaced, and remounted. "That can't be good for you, Gwendolyn. Come along."

The stream crossed his route from left to right. He turned left, therefore, and followed it uphill, allowing Gwendolyn to travel now at a walk, after her exertions.

The waterfall, when he reached it, was narrow but surprisingly high. He had to leave the stream entirely and make a wide half-circle to get up the slope to the top. When he did, he found an open area of shale on both banks, and no one in sight. He dismounted again, and let the reins trail on the ground, knowing that a well-mannered horse will be trained to stay put with the reins like that. He stood on tan flat rock in sunlight and looked down at the valley below, a green tangle dotted with those open meadows. Now and again he saw riders down there.

It was almost possible here to believe the twentieth century had never existed. Here in western Pennsylvania, less than fifty miles from Harrisburg, he could stand on this bit of high ground and look northward and see exactly what an Indian at this spot would have seen four hundred years ago. No cars, no smoke, no cities.

It was good that he hadn't left last night. Spending the one night with Mary had calmed him, had taken the edge off his rage. He was still as determined as before, but not with the same obsessiveness. A good thing to be rid of, that; it could have made him careless out of haste and impatience.

The waterfall was loud and unceasing. He never heard Recklow coming. He turned his head, and Recklow was just dismounting from a big mottled gray beside which Gwendolyn looked like a donkey.

Recklow was a man in his sixties now, but he was tall and thin and straight, and from a distance he could have been taken for a man of thirty. It was only his face that gave him away, as deeply lined and seamed as a plowed field. He'd been a ranch hand in his youth, and then a stuntman and extra in cowboy movies in the thirties and forties. He'd never had any politics, but he had personal loyalties to those he considered his friends, and when the days of the blacklist spread across the land it was inevitable that a man with Recklow's attitudes about friendship would wind up in trouble. In the early fifties he had left the West Coast and come east to Pennsylvania and bought this riding academy. It had kept him, but not very well. These days Recklow gave his loyalty almost exclusively to his horses, and took a kind of cold satisfaction in earning extra money to keep them by stepping outside the law.

He came over now to Grofield, squinting at him as though Grofield were at least half a mile away, and said, "Do I know you?" He spoke at a near shout, to be heard above the waterfall.

Grofield replied at the same volume. "I was here once with Arnie Barrow."

"I'm no good on faces....Or names either, for that matter. How'd you like Gwendolyn?"

"Fine." Grofield nodded his head toward the valley. "We played together down there for a while."

Recklow smiled for a split second with one half of his mouth. "If you come here this way, friend of this one and that one, it's guns you want. I only sell handguns and rifles. Shotguns and Tommy guns aren't my line."

"I know. I want two pistols."

"To keep on your body or in a drawer?"

"One to carry, one to keep in the car."

"To show, or to use?"

"To use."

Recklow gave him a quick sharp look. "You said that a different way." They were very close to one another, because of the difficulty of hearing.

Grofield turned his head to look toward the waterfall, as though to ask it to shut up for a while. When he looked back, he shouted, "What do you mean, a different way?"

"People that come to me are professionals. They want guns in their line of work."

"I'm in the same line of work."

"But you aren't working now."

Grofield shrugged. "No, I'm not."

Recklow frowned, and shook his head. "I don't think I want to sell to you."

"Why not?"

"A professional won't go spraying bullets around. He wants the gun to use if he has to, to show if he has to. I don't like a man to use a gun to work a mad off."

"I'm still a professional," Grofield said, pushing the words over the sound of the water. He echoed Recklow's smile of a minute ago and said, "I have to drum somebody out of the corps."

Recklow considered him, still frowning, and finally shrugged and said, "Come here."

Grofield went with him over to where Recklow had left the big gray. The horse carried saddlebags, into one of which Recklow reached, taking out three revolvers, all short-barreled and double-action. "Body guns," he said. It wasn't necessary to shout quite as loud here, farther from the drop-off. "I don't sell automatics. They're too much trouble, they don't work right." He squatted down on his heels and spread the three revolvers on the tan rock. "Look them over."

Grofield squatted down in front of him to study the guns. Two were Smith & Wesson and the third was a Colt. The Colt was the Detective Special in .32 New

Police, with a two-inch barrel. One of the S&W's was a Chief's Special in .38 caliber, the other a five shot Terrier in .32 caliber. Grofield said, "How good's the Terrier?"

"As good as the man shooting it. It'll cost you fifty dollars."

Grofield held the gun in his hand. It was very light, very small. It wouldn't be any good at a distance, but up close it would do very well.

"You want to try it?"

"Yes."

They both stood, Grofield holding the Terrier. Recklow rooted into the saddlebag again and came out with two .32 cartridges. "Fire at things in the water," he said.

"Right."

Grofield felt Recklow watching him load the gun. Recklow had the ability to make you feel you had to prove your competence to him, and Grofield was just as glad he was handling a gun of a type he'd operated before. He walked over near the stream, went down on one knee, looked around to be sure he wasn't observed, and then took careful aim at a white pebble in the stream bed up a ways to his left, away from the falls. He squeezed off a shot, a miniature geyser sprang up, and the stones in the vicinity of the white pebble jumped, roiling the water. It was hard to tell, but he thought the bullet had hit a bit to the right of where he was aiming. He might have done it himself, though, in squeezing the trigger; it was such a small gun.

He chose another target, this one near the opposite bank, and fired again. He squeezed with great care, and watched the result one-eyed, then nodded and got to his feet. He walked back to Recklow and said, "It's off to the right."

"By much?"

"Just a little."

"Consistently?"

"Oh, I could correct for it," Grofield said.

Recklow looked sour. "But you want a cut in the price."

"Well, let's take a look at one of those others," Grofield said. He hunkered down again and looked at the other two guns.

Recklow remained standing. He said, "That Terrier costs sixty-five dollars new."

"This one isn't new," Grofield said. He was still holding the Terrier while looking at the other guns, as though he'd forgotten the thing was in his hand.

"The hell with it," Recklow said. "I'll load it and give it to you for forty-five."

Grofield grinned up at him. "Done," he said. He held the Terrier out to Recklow, butt first. When Recklow took it, Grofield picked up the other two guns and got to his feet. "I'll put these away for you."

"I'll do it." Recklow stuffed the Terrier in his left hip pocket, took the other two guns from Grofield, and stood there holding them. "Now for the car. You want one in the glove compartment? Maybe a small one, too, one of these."

"No. I want to store it under the dash, I want to put a holster under there."

"Not a holster," Recklow said. "A clip."

"Have you got one?"

"Seven-fifty. It's got a spring. When you want to put

the gun away you just push it up and the clip holds it. When you want it back, you put your hand under it, push the lever with your thumb, and it pops into your hand."

"I'll take it," Grofield said. "Now, about the gun to put into it."

"You want something with more distance accuracy for outside," Recklow said. He put the two rejected body guns away, poked in the saddlebag some more, pulled out a larger revolver, and said, "Here's one. I've got a couple more on the other side." He handed the revolver to Grofield and walked around the gray to look in the other saddlebag.

The gun Grofield was holding was a Ruger .357 Blackhawk. It had the weight and heft of a solid gun, and is one of the best-looking of contemporary handguns. Looking it over, Grofield saw several short scratches, all at the same angle, on the left side of the barrel.

"Here's two more." Recklow came around the horse with a pair of guns in his hands, and stood with his palms up, displaying the guns for Grofield to inspect.

"Not the Ruger," Grofield said. "Somebody was hitting something with it." The gun on Recklow's right hand was a Colt Trooper, also in .357, with a six-inch barrel. Grofield picked it up, handed Recklow the Ruger, and studied the Colt. "This looks pretty good. What's that one?"

It was a Smith & Wesson, the model 1950 Army in .45 caliber. Grofield looked at it without taking it, and said, "Let me try the Colt."

"Of course. Hold on, I'll get you ammunition."

Grofield waited, holding the Colt, turning it over and

over in his hands, studying it. When Recklow handed him the two deceptively slim .357 cartridges, Grofield said, "I don't want to shoot into the water with these. I won't be able to see anything."

Recklow pointed across the stream, where the land continued to slope upward toward more woods. "Shoot into those rocks over there. I just don't want you to hit a customer in the woods."

"I won't."

Grofield loaded the two bullets into the Trooper, aimed at a particular fold of rock, and saw the shards fly from the exact spot he'd been pointing at. He fired the second one at once, and hit the same place. "That's good enough for me," he said, walking back to Recklow. "How much do you want for it?"

"Seventy-five."

Grofield grinned at him. "You wouldn't be tacking the five dollars from the Terrier on this, would you?"

"Seventy-five is the price," Recklow said. "I'll load it for you."

"All right."

"We'll make it five for the clip," Recklow said, as Grofield handed him back the Trooper. "That'll make it an even hundred and a quarter."

Grofield took out his wallet. He'd left the cupboard bare back at the theater to pay for this trip. He counted out four twenties, three tens, and three fives. Recklow took the money, tucked it into his shirt pocket, and said, "Ride around a while. Give me a chance to clean them up and load them and get them ready for you."

"Sure."

They both mounted and went separate ways, Recklow turning back toward the barns, Grofield deciding to head upstream a while. The water came along with little drops and pools through this stretch of tan stone, but ahead was more greenery—woods, hills. Grofield rode that way, listening to the clack of Gwendolyn's shoes on the rockface. In western movies, people rode over land like this to cover their tracks. Grofield, twisting around in the saddle, looked back and saw no mark of Gwendolyn's passage. He grinned at himself—the mighty hunter. Not out here.

4

The woman had been dead at least a couple of days. Grofield saw her lying on the kitchen floor, face down, a brown lake of dried blood forming an irregular shore about her head and extending out to make an island of one chair leg, and he didn't have to turn her over to know he would find her throat cut, or to know Myers had been here, or to know that this would be the lady of the house—Dan Leach's wife.

He had used a small screwdriver with a compartment in the removable head for several other shafts—Phillips-head, awl, and so on—to break in through this kitchen door, and now he slipped the tool away in his hip pocket and quietly closed the door. The kitchen smelled like sweet garbage. Grofield stepped over her legs, and went on through the doorway opposite to look over the rest of the house.

It was a small and neat house near Enid, Oklahoma, with a vegetable garden in the back, a farm-equipment dealer in a concrete block building for the nearest neighbor, and a straight flat two-lane concrete state highway out front. Grofield had phoned Leach here two or three times, but had never actually seen the place before. He was surprised now at how modest and small it was, and supposed that reflected Mrs. Leach's viewpoint on life, rather than Dan's. He'd had the impression Dan, when flush, liked to party, but now it seemed his wife had been a different type entirely.

Well, neither of them would do any more partying. Or cleaning. The house was almost painfully clean, so neat and orderly that the thin layer of dust that had settled since the woman's death became the place's most prominent feature, simply because it was so obviously an interloper.

Kitchen, living room, bedroom, bath. A crawl space for an attic, reached by a trap door in the bedroom ceiling and not high enough for a man to stand up straight in. A basement only barely big enough for the utilities it contained.

It was clear what had happened. Myers had come here since Grofield had seen him, knowing that Dan Leach's wife, through her brother, had been Dan's route to find him, and not wanting Grofield to be able to use the same route.

If he found the wife's brother, would Myers have been there first, too?

Grofield, in his half-dozen years working with professional thieves, had met a number of social misfit types, but he had never before met anyone so ready to kill, or so quick to assume that murder was the best answer to any problem. How many people had Myers murdered in his life and how had he managed to avoid the law so far?

And what was the brother's name? Dan had known Myers through his wife's brother. Even assuming the brother was still alive, what was his name, and how would Grofield now go about finding him?

Grofield searched the house. He found photographs of Dan and a woman who was more than likely the woman now dead in the kitchen. He found a few photographs of Dan and the woman with another man, and some with the woman and the other man without Dan, and supposed he was looking at the face of the brother. But the face wouldn't get him very far without the name.

Didn't any of these people write to each other? He searched dresser drawers and boxes on closet shelves, to no effect. A bookshelf mounted on the bedroom wall contained about thirty books, all Reader's Digest condensed volumes; he shook them out one at a time, and in the process found Dan's emergency fund, ten hundred dollar bills, five of them fluttering down from each of two books. But no names and no addresses. Grofield stuffed the thousand dollars in his wallet and left the bedroom.

The only phone in the house was in the living room, standing on the Enid directory on the end table beyond the sofa. But there was nothing written in or on the directory, and nothing but poker chips and playing cards were stored in the end table. There was no personal notebook with addresses and phone numbers anywhere around.

After a while, Grofield had to admit to himself that he was wasting his time, the house had been stripped. A woman who maintained a home like this one, small and neat and orderly, would surely have kept addresses and phone numbers neatly in a pad somewhere handy to the phone. More than that, she would surely have a Christmas card list somewhere in the house, and Grofield guessed she'd been the type who'd keep whatever letters from friends and relatives she'd ever received. That they were all gone, without a trace of search, suggested that Myers had made the woman gather up letters and address books and the like herself before he'd killed her.

Which meant it had to be done a different way; another trail would have to be found. But what about this house, and the body? Grofield's own presence here couldn't be entirely erased, so that would have to be taken care of. And, for the good of everybody Dan had worked with in the last few years, it would be best to cover up the fact of the murder itself, if he could. It was always dangerous when the police got interested in the family of a man in this business, whatever their reasons. A murder investigation here, spreading out as it would from Dan's wife to a search for Dan himself and on to a study of his former associates, could cause difficulties up and down the line.

He had come in here in the middle of the afternoon, having learned a long time ago that it's always safest to break into private homes in the daytime, accidental witnesses tending to believe that things done openly in the middle of the day are of necessity legal. He now had about two hours of daylight left.

To get started, he had to go back to the kitchen. He hated the fact of the woman lying there, face down in the lake of dried blood, and avoided looking at her as much as he could. He could only open the cellar door part way, because of her hand; the truth was, he could have pushed her arm out of the way and opened the door wider, but he preferred to use the narrow opening.

The cellar was like the interior of a submarine made of stone—small and narrow and low ceilinged and crowded with greasy machinery. Also shelves up over the sink, containing a variety of bottles and boxes and cans. Grofield went through them and found half a dozen labels that claimed the contents were flammable—turpentine, paint remover, spot remover. He carried them all upstairs, leaving the door to the kitchen open after he'd slipped through. Putting the rest of the cans on the kitchen table, he carried the rectangular quart can of turpentine with him as he went through the rest of the house, opening all the windows and being sure the doors were open between rooms. He then left a dribbled trail of turpentine from a pool in the middle of the bed down and across the bedroom floor and through the living room on a wide arc and on into the kitchen. Now the swing door had to stay open, too.

He tossed the empty turpentine can down the cellar stairs, then opened a can of paint remover and poured that all over the body. Kerosene, spot remover, everything was poured out and spread around, and the containers thrown down the cellar stairs.

The original sweet nauseating smell was gone from the kitchen now, blanketed by the sharper odors of all the things he'd spilled. Avoiding looking directly at the body as much as he could—sometimes it seemed very large, sometimes very small—Grofield pushed the wooden kitchen chairs around it, and then backed away to the exit door. He opened it, looked out carefully at the next back yard, the low wire fence, the field beyond. There seemed to be no one in sight. He nodded to himself, turned away, and went over to the stove, which was gas, of the pilotless type that needs to be lit by matches. A container of wooden matches decorated with pictures of Switzerland was hanging on the wall. Grofield took this down, held on to one match, and scattered the rest of the matches around on the floor. He turned on one of the gas burners atop the stove without lighting it, and walked back across the floor listening to it hiss. He knew that one open burner would be sufficient to cause an explosion, and that if the stove wasn't completely destroyed some sharp-eyed investigator might notice if more than one burner switch was turned to *on*.

He opened the rear door again, and the outside world still seemed just as empty of people. Standing in the slightly open doorway, he turned back to the room, struck the match on the wall beside the door, held it with the flaming end downward until it had caught well, and then tossed it gently toward the dead woman.

It didn't reach all the way, but landed on one of the wet trails on the floor. There was a tiny *phum!* and yellowish flames that were almost invisible skittered away along the trails, like ghosts of midget racers.

Grofield stepped out, shut the door behind him. He trotted away across the neat yard, jumped the low fence, and jogged around the rear of the farm-equipment dealership, leaving the way he had come. His car was a half mile down the road, in a diner's parking lot. He reached it without incident, climbed aboard, and drove away. It was a mark of how completely he thought of this as a personal thing he was on and not work that he was driving his own car, the used Chevy Nova.

He circled the area, and half an hour later he couldn't resist driving back that way to see how it had worked out. Sometimes a fire is a tougher thing to start than it should be.

A state trooper was in the road a quarter mile from the

house, directing traffic down a side road detour. Grofield stopped and stuck his head out and called, "What's the matter, officer?"

"Just keep moving," the trooper said.

"Yes, sir," Grofield said, and made the turn, following the other shunted traffic. He didn't get to see the house at all.

5

Grofield pulled the car off the road and stopped behind the tractor-trailer rig. When he got out and walked around the truck to the bank of roadside phone booths, he noticed the legend on the truck cab's door: UNIVERSAL FUR STORAGE *210–16 Pine Street Phone* 378-9825. Why was that so familiar? Then he remembered the truck in the St. Louis job, the one Hughes had bought from Purgy. It was the same company!

The same truck? No, this one was newer, the cab was newer. Grofield shook his head and went on to the booths.

The driver of the truck was in the first of the four booths, yelling his head off. Grofield couldn't make out the words through the closed glass doors, but whatever the trucker was mad about he was really mad. He had his cap clutched in his hand and kept waving it over his head as he shouted, his movements restricted by the closed-in glass walls of the booth.

Grofield went on down to the last booth at the other end, and stepped inside, leaving the door open while dialing. This was his seventh and last call, and he was making each of them from a different phone booth.

He dialed 207, the area code for Maine, and then the number. An operator came on and asked for a dollar seventy for the first three minutes. Grofield's right jacket pocket was sagging with change; he produced coin after coin to bong into the slots until he'd reached a dollar seventy. "There."

"Thank you, sir."

Then there was nothing for a long while, and then clicking, and then nothing, and then a loud click, and then ringing, and finally a woman's voice saying, "New Electric Diner."

"Handy McKay, please."

"Hold on a minute."

"Sure."

When McKay came on, Grofield said, "This is Alan Grofield. I met you with Parker a couple times, and you've passed messages on to him."

"I remember you," McKay said. "You want another message sent?"

"No. This time I'm looking for somebody else. He's in the same business I'm in, but we don't have any friends in common. I was hoping somebody I know would know how I could get in touch with him."

"I'm kind of out of touch with everybody these days," McKay said. "Except Parker. What's your man's name?"

"Myers. Andrew Myers. I'm told he did some work around the Texas area."

"I don't know him. Sorry."

"He's been traveling the last week or so with a guy named Harry Brock. Big strong guy, not very smart."

"Don't know him either. I could ask a couple of questions for you."

"I'd appreciate it."

"Where can you be reached?"

"Henrietta Motel, Wichita Falls, Texas. Area code 817, phone num—"

"Hold on, not so fast."

Grofield repeated everything, more slowly, and then

said, "I'm only going to be there till noon tomorrow."

"I'll pass the word," Handy McKay promised.

Grofield hung up and waited in the booth a few seconds, thinking about calling Mary. But he had nothing to say to her yet, and she knew not to expect him to keep in touch every day like a machine parts salesman on the road, so he left the booth and walked on around the truck and back to his Chevy. The trucker was still in the other booth, but was no longer yelling. His hand clutching the cap was at his side and he was being elaborately sarcastic now, smiling with his lips drawn back while he talked, as though in a second he'd bite the phone in half. It would be funny, Grofield thought, while the guy was on the phone, to take his truck away and drive it up to Arkansas and sell it to Purgy. Grinning, he got into the Chevy and drove away from there.

6

Grofield sat naked on the motel room bed, reading a biography of David Garrick that he'd lifted from the local library. It was after midnight, no calls had come in, and he was at the part where Dr. Samuel Johnson was describing an actor as "a fellow who claps a lump on his back, and a lump on his leg, and cries, *'I am Richard the Third'*," when the phone rang.

He hated to put the book down until he found out if Johnson had at least been put in his place, but there was no choice. Marking his place with a hotel matchbook, Grofield put the book aside, reached over to the phone, and said, "Hello?"

The voice was male, small, nasal, and guarded. "Is this somebody named Alan Grofield?"

"That's exactly the somebody this is," Grofield said.

"Huh?"

"I am," Grofield translated.

"You're looking for my friend Harry Brock."

"In a way," Grofield said.

"You sore at him?"

"No."

"You sure?"

Grofield said, "I'm sore at a guy named Andrew Myers. I think Harry Brock could tell me where he is."

"Sure he could," the voice said. "He's with him right now. I just met that Myers a couple days ago. He's a madman."

"That he is. Where'd you meet him?"

"In Vegas."

"Oh, really?"

"But they're gone from there now," the voice said. Grofield had a tendency to visualize people from their voices; in his mind, this one looked like a talking rat.

Grofield said, "Where'd they go, do you know?"

"Sure I know. But I'm not sure I want to go into it on the phone."

"Where are you calling from?"

"San Francisio."

"Then I don't think I could drop over for you to tell me in person," Grofield said.

"I don't personally have anything against Myers," the voice said. "Other than the fact that he's crazy, which is everybody's privilege, the way I see it. I wouldn't want to queer his operation."

"He's got a thing going, has he?"

"He wanted me in. It was a little too wild for me."

"Where was this?"

"Like I say, I don't want to queer things. There's him; there's the people he's got in with him."

"I'll wait till he's finished," Grofield said. "That's a promise." He was thinking, if Myers has something set up, it would be better to wait till after he pulled it anyway, and hit him when he was flush. Revenge was going to be sweet, of course, but beside that he was going to want his money back. He had a theater to open.

The rat-voice hesitated, saying, "Well, I don't know...."

"I don't know who passed the word on to you," Grofield said, "about me looking for Brock and Myers. But they must have said something about me."

"Yeah, they did."

"Whether I could be counted on or not."

"Yeah, they mentioned something about that."

"So I've told you it's not Brock I'm sore at, and I won't do anything until after they're finished doing what they're doing." The circumlocutions were a pain in the ass sometimes, but with bugging rivaling solitaire as the nation's favorite indoor one-man sport it was necessary never to be very precise about what you wanted to say.

The rat-voice said, doubtfully, "Yeah, I suppose if I call you up, I might as well go all the way."

"That makes sense," Grofield agreed.

"There's this little town in upstate New York—"

"My God!" Grofield said. "The brewery?"

"You know about it?"

"That's how I met him, too. Weeks and weeks ago. Is he still peddling that idea?"

"I didn't think that much of it," the rat-voice said seriously. "I'll tell you the truth about myself, I'm maybe not as experienced as you are. I don't want to go into my qualifications over the phone, you know, but in comparison with some of you people I'm like small potatoes. So I don't figure my attitude and my opinion count for very much. But I thought it was a little—"

Grofield let the silence go on for a reasonably long while, and then suggested, "Reckless."

"Yeah," said the rat-voice, relieved. "That's a good word. Reckless. That's why I figured I'd rather stay out of it."

"But some of the others stayed in?"

"Sure."

"Are they, uh, small potatoes, too?"

"Sure. All except Harry. And Myers."

"And they've left Vegas by now, to go up there."

"That's right."

"When do they plan to do it, do you know?"

"Pretty soon. I don't know exactly for sure."

"Well, thanks," Grofield said. "And you may not be very experienced, but you've got good instincts. That thing of his is a great one to stay away from."

"I figured that way. You know the name of the town?"

"I know it," Grofield said. "Thanks again."

"Any time."

Grofield hung up, and sat for a second smiling at the phone. "I know it," he said. He'd forgotten all about the David Garrick biography. "Monequois, New York," he said, and got up from the bed, and started to dress.

Monequois, New York

I

It was raining in Monequois. Grofield sat hunched behind the wheel of his Chevy Nova and thought about warmth and sunlight. And Mary. And the theater. And money. And Myers. And that goddam brewery across the street.

With the windows rolled up, they steamed up. With them down, cold wet wind came in. Grofield compromised—opened the vent across the way on the passenger side. The seat was getting wet over there, the windows on that side of the car were clear of steam—but not of raindrops and running water—and the windshield and side windows over by Grofield were steamed up.

So was Grofield. This was Thursday, and he remembered from Myers' briefing back in Las Vegas weeks ago that Friday was payday around here. Which meant Myers was more than likely going to hit tomorrow, or have to put it off till next week. If he was really here.

And if he was really here, where the hell was he? You can look at photographs and maps and charts, that whole suitcase full of counterspy stuff he liked to tote around with him, only up to a certain point, and after that certain point what you had to do was go around and actually stand in front of the place you were going to rob and *look* at it. Sooner or later, you would have to look at it.

So where were they? Grofield used his sleeve to remove steam from the side window for the twentieth time, and looked across the cobblestone street at the high brick wall surrounding the brewery building. There was a gate across there, and two armed private guards in gray uniforms were on that gate, and they had the kind of conscientiousness that can only come from having a paranoid employer. They checked the identification of every vehicle driver and every pedestrian to go in or out of that gate over there—every one. In the rain. Including the drivers of their own goddam delivery trucks. In the rain.

It was a part of Myers' scheme that the gang would get through that gate in a fire engine, responding to an incendiary blast that Myers would have previously set somewhere inside the building. Myers was going on the assumption that the gate guards wouldn't check IDs on firemen responding to a fire, but now that he'd seen those gate guards in action Grofield wasn't so sure he was right. And even if he was, how about that previously set blaze? An incendiary bomb with a time mechanism was a simple thing to prepare and would be a simple thing to hide somewhere in the building the day before, but just how did Myers expect to get in there to hide it? He couldn't pull the fire engine stunt twice, that just wouldn't work. So he'd have to do something else. Besides which, he or some members of the gang he'd put together were going to have to come down here and *look* at this building, they just had to. So where were they?

In the rain, he almost missed them. If Harry Brock with a chauffeur's cap on hadn't stuck his head out of the driver's window of the Rolls Royce to say something to the gate guards Grofield wouldn't have seen him at all. A chauffeur-driven Rolls had rolled up the cobblestone street and turned at the gate. Grofield had noticed the chauffeur behind the wheel and the dim figure in the back and had taken it for granted he was looking at the paranoid who owned all this. But then, when the Rolls stopped rolling and Harry Brock stuck his head out in the rain with his chauffeur's cap on to say something to the guard, Grofield became suddenly alert.

So that was Myers in the back seat, was it? The bastard was bold, that was one thing you had to give him. Myers wasn't the type to grab a lunchbucket and try to slouch in past the guard like a workman; no, his style was to show up in a Rolls Royce.

Whatever the story Myers had to go with the Rolls, it was good enough to get him through. Grofield watched the guard and Harry Brock talk, watched the guard go into his office for a minute, and watched him come back out into the rain and wave Harry Brock through. And the Rolls disappeared inside.

Grofield, sitting there, waiting for Myers to come back out, thought of an old story he'd heard one time. There was a large factory that made a lot of different products, and every day this one worker would go out the main gate pushing a wheelbarrow full of dirt. The gate guard was sure the worker was stealing something, and he kept searching the dirt, but he never found anything. After twenty years, the guard stopped the worker one day and said, "I'm retiring tomorrow, this is my last day. I can't leave this job without knowing what you're up to. I won't turn you in, but you've got to tell me. What are you stealing?" The worker said, "Wheelbarrows."

Myers and Brock were inside for nearly an hour, and there was no trouble when they left. Grofield started the Chevy and followed. Because of the rain he had to stay fairly close, but he didn't expect that to cause any problems. He was sure Myers felt safe and pleased with himself. He'd cut the route Dan Leach had taken, and he must feel he had time to run this operation and get a stake. It had been a narrow thing, Grofield getting there in time. It had needed Myers to keep pushing this plan even after an overwhelming number of professionals had told him it was no good. It had needed Myers to scrape the bottom of the barrel to find a string to work the job with him, and even then to come up with somebody smart enough to walk out. And it had needed that somebody to know somebody who knew Grofield, and who was willing to talk to him because of the friendship in the middle.

The Rolls took a turn a block from the brewery and headed toward the middle of town. Monequois was an old town with an Indian name, just a few miles from the Canadian border. It was built over and around several small but steep hills, and even the main downtown street was at a steep slant. There were no streets wider than two lanes, plus parking lanes, and the result was a perpetual daytime jam-up in the downtown area. The buildings along the main street were brick or stone, old and grimy and ugly, and the houses out around them were mostly clapboard, poor but neat. Monequois was a backwater, on no through routes, and strangers would tend to be noticed, which was the flaw in Myers' routine with the Rolls. It was a bad idea to cause attention to yourself in an area where you were going to pull a job. Grofield, the night before, had stolen a couple of New York State license plates to put on the Chevy instead of the legal Indiana plates it normally carried. The New York plates had differing numbers on them—Grofield having taken them from two different cars—but they both began *4S* and had a sequence of four more numbers after that; the likelihood that any one would notice the discrepancy was very small. And the advantage was that neither of those plates was likely to be reported as stolen. When both plates are taken from a car, the owner knows damn well he's been robbed, but when one plate is gone he'll tend to believe it fell off. He'll report the loss to the Motor Vehicle Department, but won't report a theft to the police.

The Rolls now headed directly into Clinton Street, the town's main shopping street, where traffic was stop-and-go and it could take five minutes or more to travel one block. Grofield, three cars back, composed his soul in patience and hummed melodies to the rhythm of the windshield wiper.

The Colonial Hotel was on the main street, and that was where the Rolls stopped. Myers got out, wearing a black raincoat and a black hat, and hurried across the rainy sidewalk and into the hotel. The Rolls moved on.

Was Myers actually staying at the local hotel? It was incredible the number of things the man was doing wrong. Grofield remembered Myers claiming he'd cleared the job with the local mob up here—another weird idea—and wondered if Myers thought that made him immune from the normal laws of police activity.

He would have preferred to stay with Myers now, to stake out the hotel and see what Myers did next, but there was nothing in this crowded rainy street to do with the car. Having no choice in the matter, he went on following the Rolls.

It took another quarter of an hour to get clear of downtown—it was like pulling yourself loose from an octopus—and then the Rolls turned off onto a narrow unnumbered blacktop road that took them quickly out of town and away from all other traffic. Grofield hung farther and farther back, hoping the rain would keep Brock from seeing too clearly in his rear view mirror. He knew that Brock was more stupid than Myers, but he suspected Brock was the more professional of the two. It would be Brock who would think to check the possibility that he was being followed.

Grofield wasn't sure, but he had the feeling they were now traveling north. If so, they were on their way to Canada, which was only about three miles north of town.

They traveled seven miles, taking another right turn after four, onto an even smaller and narrower road. They were traveling mostly past woods now, with an occasional rectangle of cleared farmland and an even more occasional building. There were no advertising posters, no road markers. It was impossible to tell which country they were in.

Grofield and the Rolls were the only cars in sight, and Grofield was hanging back so far now that most of the time he couldn't see the Rolls at all. He would crest a rise, come out the other end of a curve, and catch a glimpse of the Rolls up ahead. The occasional glimpse was all he wanted right now.

But the result was, he very nearly missed the turn. He came around a curve, and ahead there was a farm flanking the road. The house, on the left, had burned down some time ago, the charred sticks poking up in the rain, abandoned and desolate. The barn, on the right, had a sagging roof and some missing siding, but was mostly still in one piece. A dirt track led from the road through a gap in a crumbling fence across to the doorless wide entryway into the barn, and it was only the tail lights glowing because Brock had his foot on the brake that attracted Grofield's attention. He caught a glimpse of the two red dots inside the darkness of the barn, and quickly accelerated to be absolutely sure that was Brock in there. He took a rise, saw half a mile of road twisting and turning through a valley ahead, and it was empty of traffic.

Fine. Out of sight of the barn, Grofield turned the Chevy around and headed back. Up on the rise, he saw the barn now on his left, with the beige trunk of an automobile now jutting out the entrance. But the Rolls was black.

Grofield slowed as he went past the barn, peering at it through the rain. The driver's door of the beige car was standing open, with no one behind the wheel. Which meant Brock was in there jockeying the Rolls around, having moved the other car out of his way.

There was no question in Grofield's mind but that Brock would be heading back toward Monequois now. He drove along slowly, watching the rearview mirror, and all at once the beige car splashed into view. Grofield eased off the accelerator, slowing even more, and the beige car shot by him, arcing a sheet of water across the windshield.

It was a Buick. It had Quebec plates. Brock was at the wheel, alone in the car.

Grofield let him go on out of sight, and didn't catch up again until after the turn back onto the road that led to town. There was an occasional car or milk truck on this road; Grofield had to pass three vehicles before seeing the Buick up ahead once again.

And damned if they didn't go downtown again; Myers must have all the time in the world.

Myers wasn't alone. When they got opposite the hotel, Myers came out with two other men, and the three trotted across the street and got into the Buick. Grofield, four cars back, was pretty sure he knew neither of the other two.

The Buick kept on retracing the route of the Rolls, on out of downtown and past the brewery once more. It slowed down so much while going by the brewery that a Mustang behind it honked angrily; Grofield supposed the other two were being shown the place in person for the first time.

They went out of town to the south now, Grofield again hanging back farther and farther as the traffic dwindled, and after three miles the Buick made a right turn onto a dirt road that meandered away toward some woods. Grofield, coming slowly along the blacktop road, saw the Buick bouncing along the dirt ruts, and knew he couldn't possibly follow them in there without being noticed. Not in the daytime.

He drove on, and as he passed the turnoff the Buick attained the trees and disappeared.

2

Two A.M. Pouring. Pitch-black.

Grofield drove at five miles an hour with parking lights on across the dirt road toward the trees. The windshield wipers, whipping back and forth at top speed, couldn't keep up with the rain.

If it was still raining like this tomorrow, Myers would have to hold off on his caper. There wouldn't be any fires in Monequois, no matter how many bombs Myers set. Grofield, wishing Myers good luck up to a point, had listened to the local news at eleven, where they had said the rain would stop during the night and tomorrow would be cloudy and cooler. Grofield hoped they were right.

He reached the edge of the woods, and stopped. Turning the car around, in the dark, on this narrow dirt road, was a tricky operation. He didn't want to wind up stuck in the mud halfway; it would make for an embarrassing moment in the morning, when the boys came out to pull their job.

Grofield got it turned around at last, pocketed the keys, and very reluctantly got out of the car. That afternoon he'd done some shopping in Monequois' cramped downtown, buying himself knee-length rubber boots, water-repellent hunting trousers, a water-repellent hunter's waistlength jacket with hood, and some other things that he would maybe need a little later. Now, standing beside the car in the pouring rain, he felt that he must look like the Abominable Snowman. Or, considering the tan color of everything he had on, maybe more like the abominable mudman.

The jacket had a pouch in the front. He put his hands in there now, feeling the little Smith & Wesson Terrier and the pencil flashlight. Keeping his right hand in the pouch, fingers closed around the revolver butt, he took his left hand out with the small flashlight, switched it on, and started slogging down the faintly seen dirt road.

There was less rain in under the trees, but there was still plenty. Grofield's face and left hand were soaking wet, and despite how much he had himself closed up there were still a couple of rain trickles working their way in around his neck and down inside all the protective clothing. Feeling more and more irritable, he slogged on.

He'd traveled half a mile on foot before he came to the house. It was surprisingly large, two stories, white clapboard, and gave no sign of being abandoned. Had Myers *rented* a hideout?

Or was his place farther along? If this house were occupied now, and had nothing to do with Myers, the odds were very good the household would include a dog. Most isolated households do. Feeling very itchy about that potential dog, Grofield prowled slowly around the exterior of the house, trying to find some sign as to who, if anybody, lived there.

There was a barn behind the house, and in the barn a shiny red fire engine. Grofield shone the light on it, and smiled.

3

Grofield pressed his right hand down on the sleeping man's mouth and closed his left over his throat. The sleeper woke with an explosion of arms and legs under the covers, flinging blankets and sheets off the bed in all directions. But his shouts were turned to muffled gargles in his throat, and for all the thrashing the only sound was rustling and scrabbling—not enough to be heard through the closed door and down the hall and into any of the rooms where the others were sleeping.

There were six in the house, the same number as the gang Myers had tried to put together when Grofield first met him. They were all asleep, scattered among the four bedrooms on the second floor. Myers and this one had rooms to themselves; the other four doubled up. That was why this one had been picked; he was alone. The snoring that had covered Grofield's approach explained why.

Grofield stood on one foot, leaning all his weight on his hands, the one over the thrashing man's mouth and the one squeezing his throat. He knew this would take a fairly long while, that unconsciousness comes reluctantly when the air supply has been cut off, but the guy was helping the process by flinging himself around this way, using up the strength in his body.

Grofield had come in through the back door; Myers hadn't even bothered to lock it. Not that Grofield would have been stopped by a lock, but the carelessness of

Myers was a never-ending revelation to Grofield. It was the man's strength as well as his weakness, it made him bold and successful at the same time that it made him dangerous to be around. And ultimately, with a little help from Grofield, dangerous to himself.

The mind wakes up more slowly than the body. By the time the guy in the bed thought to attack the hands that were holding him down and cutting off his air, he had very little time or strength or consciousness left. He scratched at Grofield's gloved hands, plucked at his sleeves, tried vainly to get at his face. His arms stuck straight up, fingers moving more and more slowly, until it looked as though he were doing an imitation of an underwater plant. And his legs had stopped moving.

Grofield had searched the downstairs first, thoroughly. He had catalogued the arms supply, he had inventoried the food in pantry and refrigerator, he had observed the half dozen suitcases and bags lined up along the wall in the dining room. So they were planning to leave from here, in that highly noticeable red fire engine, and then they were planning to drive *back* here and hide out for a few days. They had food enough for at least a week. With Myers running things, the state of New York would be feeding the bunch of them within twelve hours.

Any damn fool can plot a robbery, and can get away with *planning* it. Walk in and out of the same bank every day for a month, casing it. Live where you want, drive where you want, do what you want. Any damn fool can walk into a bank or a brewery or wherever the money is—a supermarket, say—and manage to walk out again and leave the immediate scene of the crime. The part that takes the brains is not getting caught afterward. A sensible man, running this thing, would have his people in motels in Watertown and Massena, far enough away from Monequois so none of the locals will have seen them in front, to be remembered later. A sensible man would have his fire engine stashed miles from where he intends to hide out after the operation. A sensible man would keep as far away from his hideout as possible until *after* the job. A small town area like this one couldn't be hit the way Grofield and the others had hit the supermarket near St. Louis, with a large anonymous city handy to disappear into before the alarm could be raised, and a sensible man would take the local conditions into account.

Hell. A sensible man wouldn't try to knock over that brewery in the first place.

Grofield's arms were getting tired now, his fingers were growing tired from the job of forbidding this guy air. But at last, the man on the bed was running down, like a wind-up toy. His legs were stretched out like pale logs on the sheet, and his arms were collapsing downward in slow motion, the fingers sliding helplessly down Grofield's rigid arms. The madly blinking staring gulping eyes were glazing over now, the distended pupils were rolling upward. The airless heaving of the chest was growing more sporadic.

"Don't die, you silly bastard," Grofield whispered. "All I want you is unconscious."

The eyelids fluttered down. The arms fell to the sheet, flanking his still torso.

There was no sound anywhere in the house. Grofield stood unmoving a few seconds longer, listening, watching, waiting, and then very tentatively relaxed the grip of his two hands, lifted them slowly from the purpled face.

Nothing happened.

Including no intake of breath. Grofield frowned down at the unconscious man, and when breathing still didn't start he put the heel of his left hand on the guy's stomach, just over the waistband of his shorts, and leaned his weight on that hand. Lean, release; lean, release. The second time, a very scratchy sound followed it—a first breath.

Fine. So far, so good.

Grofield's eyes were used to the darkness by now, so he worked without his pencil flash while looking for the guy's clothing. He'd been sleeping in his shorts and T-shirt, and everything else was on a chair over near the door. All except the shoes, on the floor beside the bed.

Grofield took the shoes first, and removed the shoelaces. One he used to tie the guy's big toes together, and the other to tie his thumbs together behind his back. His necktie made an effective gag. The rest of his clothing, shoes, socks, shirts, pants, jacket, all went into the pillowcase Grofield stripped off the bed. A raincoat and a soft cap were in the closet, and Grofield took them, too, stuffing the cap into the pillowcase.

Next he spread a blanket on the floor, and carefully rolled the guy off the bed and down onto the blanket. He wrapped the raincoat around him as best he could, and then rolled him in the blanket. A hands and knees search around the walls of the room produced one extension cord, which Grofield tied around the middle of the long bundle he'd made. He tucked the end of the pillowcase up through his belt in the back and looped it there so the pillowcase hung down over his behind, then picked up the rolled blanket, balanced it precariously on his left shoulder, and slowly made his way out of the room.

Rain continued to pour, outside. It could be heard drumming on the roof, tapping on the windows, pouring through the gutters. The muffled, distant, soothing sounds of the rain covered the small sounds Grofield made as he carried his burden slowly down the stairs to the first floor and through the house and out the kitchen door.

It seemed darker outside the house than in, maybe because the pelting rain distorted everything you tried to look at. Grofield shifted the weight of the blanket on his shoulder and began slogging away from the house through the mud.

Halfway to the car, the figure in the blanket came to life and started to twist violently around, almost making Grofield lose his balance and fall down in the mud. He managed to stay on his feet, and when he was braced with his legs spread he took the Terrier out of his pouch, holding it by the barrel, and hit the spot on the blanket where he believed the head to be. The third time he hit it, the twisting around came to a stop. Grofield put the Terrier away again and slogged on toward the car.

4

Grofield untied the extension cord, grabbed an edge of the blanket, stood up, pulled the blanket upward, and the man inside rolled out like a college parody of Cleopatra being delivered to Caesar. The blanket was soggy, and so was the man; he lay shivering on the floor, his skin and underwear both drenched. He had a new bruise on his left cheek, probably denoting the spot Grofield had hit with the gun barrel. The necktie, once a gag, dangled limply around his neck.

He glared up at Grofield, trying to make his expression tough and unafraid, but his voice gave him away, sounding weak and frightened when he demanded, "What the hell's going on?...Who are you?...Where is this?"

"This is my hotel room," Grofield said calmly. "And you, temporarily, are my prisoner."

"I don't know what you're up to, Mac—"

"Save that speech," Grofield told him. "I know what it says. Excuse me a minute." He carried the sopping blanket away to the bathroom and hung it over the shower curtain rod.

When he came back, the guy was hunching himself across the floor toward the door. Grofield said, "You really want to go out there? Let me help." He walked past him, and opened the door. Despite the verandah-style roof over the sidewalk out front, rain swirled in with gusts of wind. The room lights glistened on the headlights and bumper of Grofield's Chevy, parked out front, but beyond it was nothing but swirling wet blackness.

The guy on the floor had stopped moving, and had hunched himself into a ball against the wind. Grofield looked down at him, shut the door, and said, "You don't really want to go out there."

"You're gonna give me pneumonia." His teeth were chattering, and he didn't have secure control of his voice.

"Not if I don't have to," Grofield said. "What's your name, by the way? I need something to call you."

"You can go to hell."

Grofield opened the door. Speaking over the sound of the storm, he said pleasantly, "I'm dressed warmer than you are. I can stand it a lot colder, and a lot wetter."

"Jesus Christ!"

"That isn't your name. Tell me your name and I'll shut the door."

"Morton!"

"First name."

"Perry!"

Grofield shut the door. "That's very good, Perry," he said. He went over to the chair where he'd dropped the pillowcase. Lifting that up now, he emptied the clothing out onto the chair—both shoes bounced away onto the floor—and went through the pants pockets till he found the wallet. He opened it, got out the driver's license, and read aloud, "Perry Morton." He turned and smiled, saying, "Very good. Truth is your best bet."

Morton was glowering at the wallet. "If you had that, why go through all that shit with the door?"

"To let you know your best move, Perry, it's to answer my questions, and to tell me the truth every time. Do you know what would have happened if I'd looked in here and it turned out your name *wasn't* Perry Morton?"

"You'd of opened the door," Morton grumbled.

"More than that. I would have pushed you outside for a minute or two, and left you there."

"Like hell. You won't let me go until you're done with me, whatever you want."

"I didn't say let you go. Perry, do you know how many other moving cars I passed on my way here from the house where I got you? None. There isn't one car out there, not one pedestrian out there. I didn't see one lit window except for a couple that were obviously night lights. It's almost three-thirty in the morning, Perry. People in a small town area like this go to bed at ten o'clock. And it's a Thursday night, a weeknight, besides. And there's a *storm* going on. Where do you think you'd go if I pushed you out there, Perry, all tied up and in your underwear? Who do you think would help you?"

Morton looked sullen, but with a trace of slyness hiding behind it. "I guess you're right," he said.

Grofield said, "I know what you're thinking, Perry. You're thinking you'll lie to me until I *do* push you out there, and then you'll hop to one of the other occupied rooms, or maybe to the motel office, and you'll get help that way. But do you know what that means? That means whoever you wake up is going to call the cops. And what are you going to tell the cops?"

"Why not tell them you kidnaped me?"

"From where? What are you doing around here? Perry, I can convince the police you're lying, I never saw you before in my life. Believe me, I can. I can make them wonder who you are and where you came from and what's going on. I can arrange it so they hold on to both of us right on through till tomorrow afternoon. You don't want the local cops asking you questions tomorrow afternoon, do you?"

"I don't know what you're talking about."

"Oh, well," Grofield said. "I hoped you wouldn't be such a slow learner." He walked over toward the door.

"Wait a second, wait a second! I didn't tell you any lies!"

Grofield stopped with his hand on the knob, and looked back. "What's going to happen tomorrow, Perry? What are you and the others supposed to do tomorrow?"

"They won't do it. When they wake up in the morning and I'm gone, they'll know something's screwed up."

"No, they won't, Perry. They'll simply think you turned yellow and ran away in the middle of the night. They're all hungry, Perry, they'll go ahead and do what they came here to do. Which is what, Perry?"

"You know everything," Morton said sullenly. "What do you ask questions for?"

"I'm lonely," Grofield said. "Also impatient." He opened the door.

"The brewery!" Morton yelled.

Grofield shut the door. "What about the brewery?"

"Jesus. We're going to knock it over. At two in the afternoon."

"For what? The beer?"

"The payroll. They've got a cash payroll."

"How many of you, Perry?"

"S-s-six."

"You cold? Listen, if you're good, and answer all questions promptly, I'll let you take a hot bath when we're done."

"I'm gonna get pneumonia," Morton said.

"Maybe not," Grofield said, carelessly. "What's the name of the guy who set it up, Perry?"

"Myers. Andrew Myers."

"And how are you going to do it?"

"We got a fire engine."

Grofield waited, but Morton had nothing else to say, so finally Grofield said, "Well, bully for you. So you've got a fire engine, so what?"

"Myers has it set for a fire to start there tomorrow. At the brewery. And we'll show up in the fire engine, that's how we'll get in."

"What about the regular fire engines?"

"We're blowing them up. Myers set that up, too, he's got a bomb in the police station. The firehouse and the police station are the same building, he's got a bomb in there to blow it up. So there won't be any other fire engine coming, and there won't be any cops chasing us when we leave."

"You're going to leave in the fire engine, too?"

"Sure."

"And go where? Back to the house where I picked you up?"

"Yeah. Not in the fire engine."

"Not in the fire engine."

"We got two cars stashed, right in town."

"Where in town?"

"There used to be a tank parts factory here, way back in World War Two. They're using the factory for something else now, but down behind it there's a warehouse and some railroad tracks they don't use any more. You know, tracks in from the regular tracks."

"A spur line," Grofield suggested.

"Yeah. They're all rusty, they're never used any more."

"And?"

"And we got two cars down by there. In the warehouse. We drive the fire engine in, we plant the other bomb, we drive the two cars out and split up and take off and meet back at the hideout."

"What other bomb?"

"We're gonna blow up the fire engine. So there's no fingerprints or clues. And to make more confusion in the town—to help us make the getaway."

"Myers has a very explosive mind," Grofield said. "So then you're going to drive the two cars back to the hideout. And then what? Wait a few days till the excitement dies down?"

"Sure."

That was another of Myers' flaws, though Grofield saw no point in mentioning it. But the kind of wave Grofield saw Myers making was not the kind of wave that died down very quickly. For at least a couple of weeks, the locals would be up in arms—vigilante groups visiting abandoned buildings; boy scouts searching the surrounding countryside; police roadblocks everywhere. If they stayed put, they'd be found. If they moved, they'd be caught. After the kind of ruckus Myers planned to make, the only thing to do was take off as fast as possible and not stop until you were separated from the scene of the crime by at least an ocean or a continent. Preferably both.

But back to another step in the plan. Grofield said, "Tell me about these two cars. What make are they?"

"One's a Buick and the other one's a Rambler."

"Colors?"

Morton frowned in confusion, but answered. "The Buick's kind of tan, and the Rambler's light blue."

"Both sedans?"

"Yeah. I don't get the point."

"You don't have to," Grofield said. "What's the plan? Three men in each car?"

"Right."

"Tell me about it."

"Well, Myers and two others in one—"

"What two others? Give me their names."

Morton looked troubled and truculent. "I don't think I ought to give you any more names. I don't know who you are or what you're up to."

"And you can tell the boys," Grofield said, "that you got your pneumonia for their sake. Assuming you ever see them again." He opened the door.

"All right!"

Grofield shut the door.

"I'll tell you," Morton said angrily. "But I'll tell you something else, too. If I ever get my hands on you, you're gonna wish you were a piano salesman instead."

"I'll remember that," Grofield told him. "But you remember something, too. When we see the way things work out tomorrow, you remember that I'm the only reason you aren't along with the rest of the boys. I'm saving you from a nice long prison sentence, and I may be saving your life. But don't thank me, just tell me who's going to be in what car."

"I wasn't going to thank—"

"You're wasting time, Perry. Tell me who's going to be in what car."

"Myers and a guy named Harry Brock and a guy named George Lanahan, they're going to be in one car, and—"

"Which one?"

"The Buick. And me and—"

"All right, that's all. What about any other vehicles? You using anything else in this caper beside the fire engine and the Buick and the Rambler?"

He shook his head. "No, that's it."

Grofield frowned, and considered reaching for the doorknob again. Instead, he said, "These bombs Myers set up in the police station and the brewery, how'd he do it?"

"What do you mean, how'd he do it?"

"I mean, how'd he get into the police station? How'd he get into the brewery?"

"I don't know. . . . I guess he just walked in."

"Both places?"

"I don't know, I guess so."

"That brewery's supposed to be a tough place to get into."

"Well, he's got the bomb in there already," Morton said. "I know that for a fact."

"How do you know it for a fact?"

"Because Myers said it was there, and we're going ahead tomorrow. I mean, *they're* going ahead tomorrow. Myers wouldn't do it if he didn't have the bomb set up, would he?"

"I guess not," Grofield said. "But what about the Rolls Royce?"

Could the bewilderment on Morton's face be assumed? Morton said, "What Rolls Royce?"

Grofield believed him, really, but he thought he ought to make sure. He sighed and said, "And you were doing so well," and opened the door.

"I don't know about any Rolls Royce! It's the truth, it's the truth!"

Grofield shut the door again. "I guess it is, at that," he said. He nodded, and went over to sit down in the second chair, the one without Morton's clothes scattered all over it. "Now," he said, "let me tell *you* something. Tomorrow, when that fire engine drives into that warehouse and you switch vehicles, the loot will go into the Buick with Myers."

"Well, naturally," Morton said. "Myers is the one running the show."

"Yes, he is. And the Rambler will drive out to that farmhouse, and stop there, and wait for the Buick, and it will never show up."

"It'll show up. What do you think we are—mugs? We chose to see who'd be in what car. I know Lanahan, he's an old friend of mine, he wouldn't cross me."

"That's right," Grofield said. "But Lanahan is going to get killed very shortly after he's out of sight of the Rambler. Because I'll tell you where that Buick is going, with Myers and Brock in it. It's going north, on a road I was on this afternoon, a back road that crosses the border without any border guard. It'll stop at a barn up there across the road from a burned-out farmhouse. Inside the barn is a black Rolls Royce. Myers and Brock—or maybe just Myers, maybe he's going to kill Brock too—will get out of the Buick, they'll take the Quebec plates off the—"

Morton started. "How'd you—"

"How'd I know the Buick had Quebec plates? I followed it into town today from that barn I'm telling you about, after Brock brought the Rolls out there. Was that you he picked up at the hotel?"

"No, two of the other guys. You been following us around all the time?"

"Just today." Grofield glanced at his watch. "Yesterday, I mean. Anyway, they'll put the Quebec plates on the Rolls, and probably at that point Myers will kill Brock. Unless he fancies Brock playing chauffeur for a day or two. They'll head north, they'll go to Montreal or Quebec, and if by any unusual chance they *are* stopped they'll have solid Canadian papers, and the loot will be stashed in the spare tire or under the rear seat or someplace like that."

"They're going to cross us," Morton said, finally beginning to believe it.

"That's right. And believe me, I think I've probably been in more of these operations than you, the cops will be all over that farmhouse hideout before sundown tomorrow."

"But they'll talk," Morton said. "None of us are real pros, except Myers and Brock. Those guys won't keep quiet, they'll tell everything they know about Myers. He doesn't dare cross them."

"I hadn't thought of that," Grofield said. "In that case, I imagine Myers will be leaving another of his time bombs behind."

"At the farmhouse?"

"Or possibly in the Rambler. That might be trickier to do, but it would more surely eliminate everybody."

Morton frowned at the opposite wall. "It makes sense," he said. "It really makes sense that way." He looked at Grofield. "I don't know what your part is in all this, but I'm glad you grabbed me out of it."

"My motivations were selfish," Grofield said.

Morton peered at him. "You're after Myers."

"I have a grudge against our friend Myers that goes back before you were born," Grofield said.

"Well, I got a grudge against him, too."

"As they say in bankruptcy court, get in line. And as they also say in bankruptcy court, they're isn't going to be much left by the time he gets to you. You want that bath now?"

"Yeah, thanks."

Grofield got to his feet. "It would be dumb to make me use the gun I have in my pocket."

"Don't worry, I'm not gonna try to do anything."

Grofield went over and squatted behind him and went to work untying the shoelace holding Morton's thumbs together. Morton, speaking over his shoulder, said, "I could throw in with you. You could use a second man."

"Not to insult you," Grofield said, "but I think I'll be better off on my own. Tough knot, this...There! Do the toes yourself."

"Sure."

Grofield sat down in the chair again, and watched Morton pick at the other lace. He said, "Maybe I'm too suspicious, Perry, but I'm not going to trust you entirely. You can take your time in the bath, and afterward I'll loan you some dry clothes, but then I'm going to have to tie you up again and lock you in the closet while I get some sleep."

"If I gave you my word—"

"I'd regretfully have to give it back. I have no use for it. Go take your bath, Perry."

Morton had finished untying the lace holding his toes together, and now he got awkwardly to his feet. "I'm in something over my head," he said. "I know I am. I won't give you a tough time. I don't know how you operate, but you don't have to kill me. I mean, I keep seeing in my mind you coming into the bathroom and holding my head under."

"Don't worry," Grofield said. "I'm not a nut. Myers is the nut."

Morton said, "I mean, that crack I made about the piano salesman and like that—"

"To tell you the truth," Grofield said, "it didn't worry me. Go take your bath."

5

Grofield parked the Chevy in the slot facing his motel room, picked up the paper bag from the seat beside him, and got out of the car.

The weather forecast had been on the button—rain ending by morning, a cool and cloudy day. The air was damp, with that post-rain chill that cuts right through clothing and flesh to strike at the bone, and the cloud-cover seemed low enough to reach up to from an attic window, but the rain had stopped, and that was the important thing.

The *Do Not Disturb* sign on the door had not been disturbed. Grofield unlocked the door, went into the room, kicked the door shut behind him, put the paper bag down on the writing desk, and went over to unlock the closet door. Morton was asleep in there, half-sitting and half-lying on the floor, head nestled on Grofield's empty suitcase. The clothing Grofield had loaned him was a little too large, and made him seem more rumpled than necessary.

Grofield leaned down and rapped his knuckles on Morton's knee. "Rise and shine, Perry," he said. "It's tomorrow."

Morton started, opened his eyes, looked around in momentary panic, saw Grofield standing over him, and relaxed as memory returned. "I couldn't figure out where I was," he said, and rubbed a hand over his face. Since it had turned out the closet door could be locked from the outside and couldn't be unlocked again from the inside, Grofield hadn't bothered to tie him up any more.

"Come on out," Grofield said. "I got us some breakfast."

"What time is it?"

"Almost noon. Check-out time here is twelve, time for you and me to get moving."

Morton got stiffly to his feet, and suddenly sneezed. "I'm coming down with something," he said.

"Probably," Grofield agreed. "Use the bathroom if you want. But don't take too long, I've got coffee here. You'll want it before it gets cold."

"I'm stiff all over," Morton said. He went off to the bathroom, walking like an old man.

Grofield called after him. "Your stuff is hanging up in there. It's dry now, change into it. I've got to pack."

"All right."

Grofield went over to the writing desk and took the things out of the paper bag. Two containers of coffee, plus sugar and milk. Four danish pastries.

Morton was only a brief time in the bathroom, and when he came out he was wearing his own wrinkled but dry clothing, and carrying Grofield's over his arm. They ate together, and Morton suggested a couple of times that he throw in with Grofield against Myers, and Grofield thanked him and declined. Morton said, "So what do you do with me?"

"I keep you around till I'm finished. Just in case in your heart of hearts you'd like to warn Myers. Or go after him yourself."

"All I want," Morton said, "is to be in some other state."

"You will be. Later."

Grofield had already paid his bill while he was out. Now, after breakfast, he finished packing and told Morton, "We'll go out together. You'll sit in front. I'll drive. If you're a clown, you'll do something to make me shoot you."

"I'm not a clown," Morton promised.

"I hope not," Grofield said. "I'll tell you something. I've fired guns in public before, and if you only fire one shot nobody ever comes to find out what it is. They think it's a backfire, or something unimportant. You've got to shoot three or four times before anybody even stops what they're doing to listen."

"I'm not going to try anything," Morton said. "You could have killed me last night when you were done asking me questions. You didn't, so I know you won't kill me now, not if I don't give you cause. So I'll just do like you say, and when you tell me I can leave I'll leave."

"That's very smart, Perry," Grofield said.

"I'm new," Morton said, "but I'm a quick study."

"I can see that."

They left the room and went out to the Chevy. Grofield put his suitcase on the back seat, he and Morton got in front, and he drove away from there, heading for the barn where he'd last seen the Rolls Royce.

It was nearly one thirty when they reached the barn. Morton said, "Is that it?"

"That's it. The Rolls is inside."

"That Myers," Morton said. "He's really something."

"Not for long."

Grofield braked almost to a stop. A driveway went up to the left, toward the burned-out house; originally, there'd been an attached garage. Grofield made the turn into the driveway, drove up it, angled off onto shaggy lawn, and drove around the house to where a swing and a slide showed that children had lived in this house once. Grofield pulled to a stop behind the section of the house that was still jutting up the highest—bits of wall and up-ended beams not much higher than a man. But enough of it to hide the Chevy from the road.

"Last stop," Grofield said. "Everybody off."

They both got out of the car, and Grofield got the length of clothesline from the floor in back. Morton, seeing him come around the car with it, said, "What's that for?"

"To keep you safe while I'm busy."

"You don't have to tie me up."

"Yes, I do, if I don't want to distract myself. Come on, Perry, don't get difficult. We've got a nice relationship going."

"I don't want to get tied up!"

"Perry, it'll be worse if I have to hit you with the gun butt."

"Tell me what you're going to do."

Grofield pointed to some trees farther up the hill behind the house. "Tie you to one of those. I'll come back and let you loose again afterward."

"I don't like that," Morton said. His eyes were wide, and his voice had started trembling again.

"It won't be for long. Maybe an hour. And you're dressed nice and warm now, with your raincoat and all. Come on, Perry, don't make things tough for yourself."

"I just don't like it, that's all," Morton said, but there

was no fight in him now, and when Grofield took the Terrier out of his pocket and gestured with it, Morton went grudgingly on up the hill.

The trees were old, not very tall, but very thick in the trunk. Grofield tied a knot around one of Morton's wrists, then pulled the rope partway around the tree and tied his other wrist. When he was done, Morton was standing with his arms around the tree as though embracing it. The trunk was too thick for him to get his arms all the way around it, and the foot or so between his wrists was where the clothesline was stretched across.

"I've got to stand here like this?"

"It won't be long," Grofield promised again. "I'll come back up when I'm finished with Myers."

"Good Christ!" Morton cried, turning his head, craning his neck so he could see Grofield. "What if you lose?"

"Then I'd say you're probably in trouble," Grofield told him.

6

Two thirty-five. A slight drizzle had started, polka-dotting the surface of the road. Grofield, up in the hayloft, looked at his watch, looked out the opening in the wall at the road, and wondered if he'd made a mistake somewhere. Could Myers really have meant to go back to that farmhouse? But he'd stashed a car here that none of the others had known about; he'd arranged to split the group into two cars with the profits in his; he *had* to be planning to come here.

Of course, it was also possible they'd been caught. The operation Myers had worked out was so full of speed and explosions and terror and boldness that it ought to work, at least long enough for them to make their initial getaway, but it was always possible something had gone wrong and they'd all been caught. Particularly with the semi-pros Myers had been reduced to working with. And particularly with Myers being the unpredictable wild man he was.

Poor Perry, Grofield thought, looking out at the drizzle. He really will get pneumonia, the poor bastard.

If nothing happens by three o'clock, he told himself, I'll go over and listen on the Chevy's radio and see what I can find out. Listen to the three o'clock news.

A car was coming. Grofield glimpsed it a long way off, rounding a curve two or three hills from here; up here in this hayloft he had a pretty good view of the countryside, and one small pie slice of distant road could be seen down past a farmer's field in that direction.

The right car? It had been moving fast, and it seemed to be the right color. The uncertain drizzle didn't affect vision the way yesterday's downpour had, but the distance, the car's speed, and the narrow slice of visible road all combined to make him less than completely sure.

It was the right car. It came around the final curve less than half a minute after his first glimpse of it, and it was being driven very very hard. The curve topped a rise, and the beige Buick came off the rise with all four tires for one split second off the ground, as though a stunt driver were at the wheel. When it hit, it slued badly, rocking from side to side on its springs as the man at the wheel fought to keep the thing under control. He wasn't really a stunt driver after all.

No, he was just a fool. The way he took the turn off the road toward the barn, the Buick really should have tipped over. It wanted to, it hung for a long streaming second on the very edge of imbalance, and then it slammed down on its right side tires again and headed full-speed for the barn.

Grofield fully expected the damn thing to crash into the barn like a bowling ball into the pins, and he braced himself to try to leap clear of the wreckage when the barn collapsed. But then the Buick's brakes squealed, the car slued badly again to the right, and it came to a stop sideways to the barn door, no more than two feet from a collision. Despite the light rain, the arrival managed to raise a cloud of dirt, which slowly settled on the Buick's windshield and hood.

Meanwhile, the driver's door burst open and Harry Brock lunged out, yelling at the top of his lungs: "—think you're so damn smart, you can drive it yourself! Drive the goddam Rolls yourself! Do every goddam thing yourself! You're *smart,* you are!"

The Buick was so close to the barn that when Myers jumped out the passenger side he wound up within the barn doorway and out of Grofield's sight. But Grofield could hear him: "You got *blood* on me, you lunatic! Driving like that!"

"You had to kill him in the car! Smart again!"

Myers came running around the front of the Buick, not to attack Brock physically but to shout at him from closer range. "Now everything's *my* fault! I did my part!"

"Yes, you did. You're full of hot air, Andy, nothing but hot air."

Myers was obviously trying to get control of himself. "Harry, we can't stand around here arguing with each other. There'll be roadblocks up, there'll be police all over the place. Harry, we've got to switch the plates and put the Buick in the barn and blow it up, and we don't have *time* for all this."

"Do it yourself," Brock said, and turned his back on Myers to walk away across the grass, paralleling the road. "I'm done taking orders from a jerk like you."

"Harry, we *need* each other!"

"I need you like I need a hole in the head," Brock said, turning around to put his hands on his hips and glare at Myers. It was a strangely womanish gesture, making him look like a fishwife in a street brawl.

Myers went running after him again. "Harry, we can't waste the *time!*"

Brock made a disgusted pushing-away gesture with both arms, and turned his back again.

Myers caught up with him, and reached out to grab his arm. "Harry, listen to me, we can't—"

Brock spun around and punched Myers in the face. Myers staggered backward, lost his balance, and fell heavily on his rump. He sat there, obviously dazed, and Brock stood over him and said, "You don't touch me, you big-talking jerk. What are you good for, anyway? You just screw everybody up. And I'll tell you what I'm going to do. I'm going to leave you right here. Give me my half of the money, I'm taking the Rolls. You can keep the Buick, *with* the plates. And you can have George, too, and do what you want with him."

Grofield was very interested in that speech. The way they'd been bickering, he'd been afraid the robbery hadn't worked out after all, they hadn't managed to breach the brewery gate with their fire engine. But with Brock demanding his share of the money, the argument had to have some other cause.

Could it just be tension, nervousness, no real reason to fight at all? Grofield had seen people get into deadly arguments over nothing at all just after a difficult job, this could be the same thing.

Down below, Brock had decided to help himself to whatever Myers was carrying on his person. He stood over Myers, bending down to poke his hands into Myers' coat pockets, and all at once Myers moved, a sudden blur of confused motion—Brock yelped, a weird high-pitched sound, and hopped backward on one leg. Blood was spurting from high on his other leg, very near the groin, streaming out through a new ragged slit in his trousers.

"You cut me! You cut me!"

"You son of a bitch, I'll do better than that." Myers got

to his feet, a little shaky, waving the knife in his right hand. Where it had blood on it, it was dull, but where raindrops had landed on it it glistened.

Brock hobbled away in a frantic circle, hopping backwards, clutching the top of his thigh with one hand, trying to hold his blood in. "What were you trying to do?" he cried. His voice was still high and strange.

"Stand still, Harry," Myers said, stalking him, "I'll show you what I'm trying to do." And he lunged forward, aiming the knife at Brock's stomach.

Brock flailed at the knife with his hands, in panic and fear, and was very lucky. Both hands were cut, but the knife suddenly flipped away from Myers' grip, and the tide had turned again.

Myers leaped for the fallen knife. Brock, standing on his good leg, swung the hurt one as though trying for a fifty-yard field goal. His shoe caught Myers high on the chest and sent him sailing in a complete somersault through the air. Myers landed on his back, and rolled, and Brock came up with the knife.

Myers ran into the barn. Grofield, trying to see, stuck his head as far out the hayloft opening as he could, but Myers was completely within the barn. And now Brock was going in after him, limping badly, holding his wounded leg with one hand and holding the knife out in front of him with the other.

The next part, Grofield didn't see. He stayed crouched in the hayloft, the Terrier in his hand, watching the ladder he'd come up and listening to the sounds from down below.

There was no sound at all at first, except the slight dragging rustle of Brock's wounded leg as he moved across the barn floor. Then, in a wheedling soft voice, Brock saying, "Where are you, Andy? Come on out, Andy, come get your knife back."

Then there was silence, total silence, for almost a minute. Grofield strained his ears and his eyes. There was nothing from down there. He looked over his shoulder at the opening in the front wall, half-expecting to find them both behind him, but he was still alone up there. He kept on having the feeling, though, that they were up there with him, both of them, just out of his sight.

The scream was preceded by a sudden rush of footsteps, and followed by a confused banging and scuffling. Something clattered, and then Myers sounded off with a jagged frightened half-crazy laugh, crying, "You don't like the pitchfork, huh? You don't like it, huh?"

Silence for a few seconds. Another rush of scuffling and footsteps and panting, but no scream this time. And then silence. And then Myers, terrified, screaming, *"No!"* Metal clanged against metal, there was running, something metal falling, and then vibration in Grofield's feet, and Grofield started, staring at the ladder. Somebody was coming up.

Myers. He was bleeding from two long cuts on the face, his clothing was torn, he looked as though he had other cuts on his body, and he scrambled practically all the way up to the hayloft before he saw Grofield squatting there, pointing the Terrier at him. Then he yelled, not like a man who's been hurt but like a man who's seen a ghost, and he shoved himself backwards out into the air away from the ladder, and plummeted out of sight.

Did that growl come from Harry Brock? A growl of

satisfaction and victory. Grofield hunched himself smaller, and didn't move.

Below, Myers was babbling at the top of his voice. "It's Grofield, Harry! It's Grofield up there! We need each other.... We've got to help each other.... We've got to get Grofield! Harry! *Harrreeeeeee!*"

The next sounds were chunky, and the silence after them seemed moist. In that silence, Harry Brock said, "Grofield? You really up there, Grofield?"

Come and look, Grofield thought, pointing the Terrier at the ladder.

"Well, let's make sure," Brock said, down below. "Let's be on the safe side."

Grofield waited. The floor beneath him seemed paper thin. His lips were dry. All he could hear was raindrops hitting leaves of grass.

A crash shook the barn. Another one. The top of the ladder, which had been nailed in place, fell away.

"There," Brock said, down below. "You up there, Grofield? You don't have to say anything. You're up there, you can stay there."

Grofield didn't move.

"Now, you son of a bitch," Brock said, "where's the money?" So he was searching what was left of Myers. Grofield thought of creeping forward to the inside edge of the loft and looking down into the barn, but was afraid to move. This floor was noisy. Neither Myers nor Brock had used a gun, but Brock might have one. A sound from up here, and Brock would know exactly where Grofield was. A bullet coming up through the floor between Grofield's legs was not a pleasing thought.

What was happening down below? Small sounds, undecipherable. Grofield waited, and didn't realize what Brock had in mind until he heard the Buick door slam out front. The passenger side door, facing the barn opening, left open by Myers when he'd jumped out of the car.

Now Grofield did move, and fast. He straightened, turned, ran one long pace, and jumped feet first out through the hayloft opening.

It was about six feet to the top of the Buick. Grofield landed, the top buckled under him, his shoes slid on the wet metal, and he fell heavily on his hands and knees, facing the rear of the car.

He couldn't get a purchase. He slid backwards despite himself, and knew his legs were dangling down in front of the windshield. The only thing to do was push hard, and slide his whole body down across the windshield and onto the hood.

Lying on his stomach on the hood, he stared through the windshield at Brock, who stared back pop-eyed. Grofield pulled his arm up in front of his face, fired at Brock through the windshield, and Brock yelped and heaved himself out of the car on the driver's side. Grofield fired at him again as he was getting out and saw the puff on the shoulder of Brock's coat.

But Brock kept moving. He ran away from the car, and Grofield pushed himself off the hood and onto his feet. Turning, he saw Brock go stumbling around the corner of the barn, and made after him.

Brock was on his knees beside the barn, leaning his right shoulder against it, his head bowed. Grofield circled him cautiously, and Brock lifted a very sleepy face. "It was all Myers' fault," he said. He mumbled it, as though he'd been drugged.

Grofield said, "Where's the money?"

"In my pocke'. Co' pocke'."

"A hundred twenty thousand dollars? In your coat pocket?" That, according to Myers, was the size of the payroll at the Northway Brewery.

Surprisingly, Brock began to laugh. The agitation disturbed his balance, and he fell forward onto his face, and was quiet.

Grofield rolled him over, and Brock looked up sleepily. His eyelids were heavy, he was having a tough time keeping them up. Grofield said, "What's funny? Where's the hundred twenty thousand? Didn't the caper go?"

"They pay by check!" Brock started to laugh again, but it seemed to hurt him, and he just smiled. "They went back to checks," he said sleepily, his smile looking lazy and good-natured. "They couldn't do the cash, they went ba…" His eyes closed.

Grofield poked his shoulder. "What did you get?"

"Twenny-seven hunnnn…"

"Twenty-seven hundred dollars?"

Brock was snoring.

Grofield went through his coat pockets, and there it was. Twenty-seven hundred dollars, in large bills. Petty cash, probably, the only cash they keep in the place. Six men, a fire engine, three getaway cars—twenty-seven hundred dollars.

"He didn't make sure," Grofield said. He shook his head, and stood up, and Brock stopped snoring. Grofield looked down at him, and he wasn't breathing at all. Grofield turned away and went back around to the front of the barn to make sure.

There was nothing in the Buick but a dead body

in the back seat. That would be Lanahan.

There was nothing in the Rolls parked inside the barn except three suitcases in the trunk, and they contained clothing and toilet articles and things like that.

Finally, Myers. Brock had apparently decided to make him leak to death, and had used both the knife and the pitchfork for the job. It was impossible to search the clothing without getting bloody fingers. Grofield grimaced with distaste as he went through the pockets, and his revulsion was such that he almost missed the money belt entirely. But he found it, and untied it, and pulled it off Myers' body.

It had four compartments. Two of those, on the left side, had been punctured, and were soggy with blood. Grofield didn't open them at all. He opened the other two, on the right side, and there was the money.

His own money. It still had the Food King wrappers on it. The remains of Grofield's piece of the supermarket job. He sat down on the floor and counted it, and there was four thousand, one hundred eighty dollars there. Out of thirteen thousand, three hundred twenty-five that Myers had taken away from him.

"It's something, anyway," Grofield said aloud, and stuffed the money into his pockets. Going across the road and up toward the Chevy, he added twenty-seven hundred and forty-one hundred eighty in his head, and came up with six thousand, eight hundred, and eighty dollars.

"We can open anyway," he said. He walked around the corner of the burned-out building, and a charred piece of two-by-four came around in a fast arc, hissing it was moving so fast, and hit him square in the face.

7

Grofield sat up and touched his nose and his hand came away bloody. He could barely see, the way his eyes were puffed shut, and the whole front of his face was stinging. Also, he had a violent headache.

He looked down at himself, and he was sitting on the ground beside a burned-out house in a light rain. And his pockets had all been turned out; he'd been rolled. He said, "Hey."

Movement attracted his attention. He turned his head, slowly and carefully, and there was a man standing beside a car. Grofield's car, the Chevy. And the man was—son of a bitch, it was Perry Morton!

Morton had been just about to get into the car, but now he stood there looking at Grofield and said, "You awake already? I figured you were good for a couple hours."

"How long—" His throat felt raspy; he cleared it, and started again. "How long was I out?"

"Maybe five minutes. Just long enough for me to get your money and your gun and your car keys." Morton was feeling pleased with himself, and why not?

Grofield cleared his throat again. "Don't leave me here, Perry," he said. "This area's going to fill up with cops. I gave you a break, you give me one."

Morton considered. But he was feeling so smug and pleased with himself, he had to be magnanimous. He said, "If you can make it to the car, I'll take you along."

"Thanks, Perry," Grofield said.

It took him two tries to get to his feet, and then he was dizzy as hell. He staggered over to the passenger side of the Chevy and climbed in beside Morton, who had just started the engine.

Morton looked at him and grinned. "Just remember I've got the gun now," he said. "I'll expect you to be as smart with me as I was with you."

"I'll remember," Grofield said.

Morton started the car, and headed them away from there. "I'm going farther up into Canada, and then I'll head west."

"Fine with me." There was a make-up mirror on the sun visor on the passenger side; Grofield put the visor down now and studied his face in it. His nose didn't seem to be broken, but he had several little cuts on both the nose and cheeks. Also he was going to have two lovely black eyes, but they'd be gone before the season started.

"Lemons never lie," Grofield said, and sighed.

"What was that?"

"Nothing."

They drove in silence a while, and then Morton, smiling, said, "Well, you're the bigtime pro and I'm just the new boy, but I guess I'm a fast learner, huh?"

"You sure are," Grofield said. He'd licked a handkerchief and was wiping the blood off his face. It was just as well to have a chauffeur for the rest of today, until they were a good distance from the robbery area. There was no hurry about taking the reins back. The Colt Trooper under the dashboard would keep.

Morton turned the radio on, and began to whistle along with the music.

Grofield put his handkerchief away and said, "Wake me when the news comes on, will you?"

Morton glanced at him in surprise. "You're going to sleep?"

"I've had a hard day," Grofield said.

"Well, you can sure rest now," Morton said, and gave a broad smile.

"Yes, I can," Grofield said, and closed his eyes. The Chevy drove across Canada into the sunset.